C. ALEXANDER LONDON

SCHOLASTIC INC.

If you purchased this book without a cover, you should be aware that this book is stolen property. It was reported as "unsold and destroyed" to the publisher, and neither the author nor the publisher has received any payment for this "stripped book."

No part of this publication may be reproduced, stored in a retrieval system, or transmitted in any form or by any means, electronic, mechanical, photocopying, recording, or otherwise, without written permission of the publisher.
For information regarding permission, write to Scholastic Inc., Attention: Permissions Department, 557 Broadway, New York, NY 10012.

ISBN 978-0-545-47706-2

Copyright © 2013 by C. Alexander London
All rights reserved. Published by Scholastic Inc.
SCHOLASTIC and associated logos are trademarks and/or registered trademarks of Scholastic Inc.

10 9 8 7 6 5 4 3 2 13 14 15 16

Printed in the U.S.A. 40
First printing, March 2013

For my grandparents

"Cry 'Havoc!' and let slip the dogs of war . . ."
— Mark Antony in *Julius Caesar* by William Shakespeare

"You can read every day where a dog saved the life
of a drowning child, or lay down his life for his master.
Some people call this loyalty. I don't. I may be wrong,
but I call it love — the deepest kind of love."
— Wilson Rawls, *Where the Red Fern Grows*

NO SNOW IN THE DESERT

"Hey, Rivera," Goldsmith whispered in my ear. His breath frosted the air between us. "Looks like some kind of fairy tale out there in the woods, don't it?"

Crunchy snow clung to the tree trunks like white fur. I pressed my fingers against the ground in front of me and the snow crackled. I stood up to my shoulders in the icy foxhole. Goldsmith stood beside me, shivering and talking too much.

"I feel like Little Red Riding Hood's gonna come through the forest any second." He laughed. "Off to grandmother's house she goes. Except, she ain't finding no grandmother out here. Just us, the GIs of the Ninety-Ninth Infantry!" He slapped the snow in front of him and laughed again.

I grunted. I didn't think we were supposed to be talking. We were supposed to be watching the forest for Krauts — I mean Germans, German soldiers, Hitler's army. Everyone said the Germans were as beaten as the St. Louis Browns in the World Series, that the war in Europe was about over. Everyone said we'd be home by Christmas.

I didn't want to be home by Christmas. I had just gotten here and I wanted to fight the Nazis, not sit in a frozen foxhole with some guy jabbering in my ear all morning. I kept my eyes fixed on the woods in front of me. The snow wasn't so thick. I could see branches and a few scraggly bushes poking up from the ground, covered in frost, like icing on a cake.

I doubted I'd see anything more exciting than that. They sent the new guys, replacement soldiers like me, out here to the Ardennes forest in Belgium precisely because it had been so quiet. There was little risk that my lack of experience would mess anything up or get anyone killed here.

I couldn't feel my feet in my boots anymore. I hoped they were still there below me. I kicked them against the frozen dirt just to be sure. They stung.

"Hey, Rivera," Goldsmith pressed me. "You hearing me? Do you speak English, even? Huh? You *habla inglés*?"

I rolled my eyes and tried to ignore him.

Goldsmith's rifle lay between us, propped up against the edge of the foxhole, next to my medic's bag. I knew that if he had to use his rifle, I'd probably have to use my medic's bag. I'd had just a few weeks of first-aid training before the Ninety-Ninth Infantry called me up and dropped me down here on the front lines as a replacement soldier the previous night. I didn't even know what unit I was in. A sergeant had simply put me in this foxhole next to Goldsmith in the pitch black and told us to look out for Germans.

"What we do if they show up, Sarge?" Goldsmith had asked.

"Shoot them," the sergeant grumbled, and stalked away into the cold night.

Goldsmith probably knew as much about fighting the Nazis as I knew about being a medic in a war, but we were stuck together in the foxhole all night, so we both did our jobs and looked out for Germans. I kind of wished I had a rifle instead of a bunch of bandages and a big red cross on my arm.

In boot camp, all the guys had made fun of me for training to be a medic instead of a rifleman, but it wasn't my fault. I *wanted* to fight Nazis. That's why I joined the army in the first place, to show that I was a fighter, that I could be heroic, but the army didn't ask what I wanted when they gave me my assignment.

I scanned the dim forest, shivering through my thin coat, but I didn't see anything to make me worry. Somewhere in the night a heavy artillery barrage cut loose. A lot of firepower. The ground vibrated beneath us, even though the attack was miles away.

I figured it was our guys, way down the front line — but how far, I couldn't tell. I figured I wouldn't want to be the Germans fielding those incoming shells. I almost felt bad for them. Except they were Nazis, so I figured they were getting what was coming to them.

I hugged myself and rubbed my shoulders to keep warm. My fingers squeezed the checkerboard patch on my shoulder, the insignia of our division. The Ninety-Ninth. They called us the Battle Babies because by 1944, we still hadn't seen real combat. There had been some fighting a few days back, while I was still in France on my way to the front. I was disappointed to miss it. It was bad enough to be in the war without a weapon, but if I never got the chance to be in a battle, how would I ever hold my head up high back home? It felt like high school baseball all over again. I rode the bench in baseball, and now I was riding the bench in the Second World War.

"Rivera!" Goldsmith whisper-shouted at me, fed up with my silence. "I asked if you speak English."

"Yes!" I snapped at him. "I speak English."

"You ain't said a word all night. I thought you might only speak, what? Spanish?"

"I do speak Spanish," I told him. "And English."

"You Puerto Rican?"

"American."

"We're all American . . . but where you from *before* America?"

"I was born in America," I told him.

"You know what I mean."

"My parents are Mexican," I told him, and looked away. I didn't want to see his face. There'd been riots last year all over the country and a lot of people blamed the Mexicans for them. I didn't have anything to do with that stuff, but some people still just didn't trust anyone who spoke Spanish.

But I *was* American, through and through. Why else would I be freezing my behind off in a foxhole in Europe? "I'm from Albuquerque."

"I'm from New York," Goldsmith said. "We got a lot of Puerto Ricans."

I didn't feel like explaining how Puerto Ricans and Mexicans were totally different, so I just shrugged.

"My family's from Lithuania," he continued. "Eastern Europe, you know?"

"Uh-huh," I said, although I wasn't sure what the question was. Goldsmith loved to talk. I was happy to just keep quiet in the early morning light and watch the forest, but he was determined to have a conversation.

"They got chased out for being Jews," he said. "Their homes and businesses burned down, even their synagogue. So they came to New York. Started over. Garment business, right? I guess you figured that."

"Uh-huh," I said again. What did *I* know about New York or Jews or the garment business? I grew up in Albuquerque, New Mexico, played ball in high school, and signed up for the army before I even graduated. I didn't figure anything about anything, except that I was going to fight for my country and I was the only guy in my class going so soon. Other guys in school were bigger and stronger and tougher than me, but they all just sat around waiting for the draft, or waiting for the war to be over. Not me. I didn't wait. I even lied about being eighteen so that I could enlist. I wouldn't be eighteen for another two months, but with Hitler losing the fight, I didn't think I could wait. If the war ended before I got in it, I'd never be able to show just how tough I could be.

"You don't say much, huh?" Goldsmith shook his head.

"Not much to say," I told him.

"You got a problem with me being Jewish?"

That took me by surprise. As far as I knew, I'd never met a Jewish guy before. Was I *supposed* to have a problem with him being Jewish?

"I don't have a problem with that," I told him. "You got a problem with me being Mexican?"

"You said you were American," he smirked. That broke the tension. We both laughed a little. I guess each of us was used to people having a problem with who we were. Now that we were together in this frozen little foxhole in this frozen forest, ordered here by the Ninety-Ninth Infantry Division of the United States Army, the only people we had a problem with were the Nazis.

And we were here to kick their butts all the way back to Berlin.

"Check it out." Goldsmith reached under his shirt and pulled out his dog tags hanging on a chain around his neck. Stamped into the thin metal was his name and the serial number the army had given him, and then the letter *H*.

"For *Hebrew*," he said. "So, you know, if something happens to me they know what kind of prayers to say and stuff."

I nodded. I didn't like to think much about that kind of thing, but I knew it was there. That's part of the medic's job. In case a guy we were treating . . . well. I had a *C* on mine, for *Catholic*. If anything happened to me, they'd call a priest. I didn't know who a Hebrew guy would want called. The woods were so quiet, I didn't figure it would come to that.

"When we get to Berlin, I can't wait to show this to those Nazis." He laughed. "The Nazis think we Jews are nothin'. They think they can just kick us around, bully us, but I'll show 'em. They'll know it was a Jew who beat them."

"I thought you said we were all American?" I cracked a smile at him.

"I'm a New Yorker," he said, laughing. "We're something else all together. Nobody kicks us around. We'll teach Hitler what's what. You and me!"

I nodded. We fell back into a comfortable silence, the chattering of our teeth the only sound I could hear. The sun was just starting to rise. After a few minutes, I guess the quiet got unbearable for Goldsmith, because he started up the whispering again.

"You even know the Little Red Riding Hood story?" he asked me. "I mean, do they have fairy tales in Mexico?"

"Albuquerque's in New Mexico," I said. "And yes, we have fairy tales."

"Your *abuela* tell them to you?" he smirked. *Abuela*. Grandmother. I guess Goldsmith knew some Spanish. "Like I said," he explained. "We got a lot of Puerto Ricans in New York. I picked up a few things."

"Mi abuela me dijo un montón de cuentos," I tried, but he just stared back at me blankly. Guess he didn't pick up *that* much Spanish from his Puerto Rican friends. "Yeah," I told him in English. "My grandmother told me a lot of stories, but they were different from Little Red Riding Hood. Old ones from the little village where she grew up."

"Hey, we got that in common." Goldsmith smiled. "My grandma told me old ones too, from her little village. She only speaks Yiddish, so I never really understood much of what she said."

"What's Yiddish?"

"It's an old Jewish language," he said. "You never heard of Yiddish?"

"No," I said.

I don't know why, but it felt kind of good to be in this frozen little foxhole with another guy whose grandmother spoke to him in a different language. It made me feel less like I was different from all the other guys. At basic training, nobody else spoke Spanish or talked about old folk tales or missed the tamales their grandmothers made.

The thought of fresh tamales made my mouth water. Army food wasn't good, and out here on the front, there wasn't much of it. I was already hungry.

I wanted to ask Goldsmith what kinds of food his grandmother made for him, but he asked me a question first.

"So, down in *New* Mexico, you got snow like this?"

"Nothing like this," I told him.

"You live in, what, the desert?"

"It's not really the —"

He didn't let me finish.

"I guess it don't snow much in the desert," he chuckled. "You know my people originally came from the desert. The Hebrews. Spent forty years wandering in the desert in ancient times. Must have been awful, but at least there wasn't all this snow, right? I'm freezing my schnoz off."

I just wrinkled my forehead at him. I didn't want to be rude, but I couldn't really follow what he was talking about.

"*Schnoz* means nose in Yiddish," he said. "Like Jimmy Durante, the Great Schnozzola?"

I shrugged. I knew Jimmy Durante was some kind of performer, but I followed baseball, not singing and dancing.

"Oy, *boychick*, we gotta give you some culture." Goldsmith shook his head and rolled his eyes at the sky.

"What's *boychick*?" I asked.

"It's like saying *kid*," he explained.

"Like *vato* in Spanish?" I asked.

"*Vato*?"

"Just, like, a guy, a pal," I said.

"Vaaa-to, va-to, va-va-va-vato." Goldsmith played the word around in his mouth, stretched it, rolled it around. I guess we had something else in common aside from our grandmothers and their old stories. We both liked languages.

"So, *vato*," he asked. "You wanna learn some Yiddish?"

The morning was pretty boring so far, so I told him sure I would. Maybe learning a few new words would pass the time. Now that we were talking, I realized it was definitely better than sitting in freezing silence, waiting for something to happen.

"Ok, I guess *yutz* is as good a place as any to start," Goldsmith said.

"What's it mean?"

"A *yutz* is like a fool," he explained. "Like us!" He laughed and slapped at the icy ground in front of him. "Standing in this cold foxhole all night because some generals say we got to. Or, like Hitler, thinking he can beat the whole world in a fight. He's a *yutz* and a half."

"Yutz," I repeated to myself. It was a fun word, felt good in the mouth, even though it was, I guess, kind of an insult.

"So you got some more Yiddish you can teach me?" I asked. "I can't just go around calling everyone *yutz* all the time. I don't want to get —"

"Shh!" He cut me off and grabbed his rifle. He ducked low. I ducked down beside him, so just our eyes and the barrel of his rifle poked above the top of our foxhole. We listened to the forest.

I couldn't hear anything at first. Then there was a loud slap, like a book dropped onto the floor in a silent study hall, and then a whistle in the sky.

"Incoming! Take cover!" someone shouted from another foxhole down the line. I hadn't even known there were any other foxholes up there with us. When I leaned up to try to see who had shouted, Goldsmith yanked me back down just in time for the ground in front of us to explode.

Then another slap, a whistle, and another explosion.

A tree above us burst into flames and smoke, branches crashed onto the crunchy snow of the forest floor. Goldsmith jumped up and raised his rifle. My ears were still ringing and I stayed at the back of the foxhole for a second, kind of in shock. If Goldsmith hadn't pulled me down, I would have died.

He had just saved my life.

"Thanks!" I yelled, but he didn't hear me over the crack of his rifle and the whistle of the artillery.

The Germans were attacking.

RED SNOW

Goldsmith returned fire.

I couldn't even see where he was aiming. His bullets shaved the snow off the trees and splintered their bark. More bullets buzzed in our direction, like a swarm of dragonflies racing one another overhead. I felt silly just standing there beside him with nothing to do.

Another high-pitched whistle sounded, and we both ducked down into the foxhole. I tried to imagine myself small, like a little bug curling up into my helmet, squeezing my entire body into it. Then artillery shells hit with loud explosions, one after the other.

Boom! Boom! Boom!

Goldsmith and I squeezed together beneath a rain of dirt and snow. We pressed together in the tiny foxhole, side by side, hugging each other tighter than I'd ever hugged anyone in my life. My ears rang. It felt like an earthquake rumbling underneath us as the explosion rocked the ground. Smoke burned my eyes and my nostrils.

Seconds after the shelling stopped, I heard a shout from somewhere down the front line, from some other foxhole. "Medic!" a voice called out, pleading, screaming. "Medic!"

"Hey, *vato*." Goldsmith let me go and met my eyes. "I think they need you."

He popped up and started shooting once more. I peeked out and saw that the forest in front of us was in chaos. Tall trees had fallen this way and that, like they'd been knocked down by an angry giant. Dirt and mud and deep craters broke the once-untrodden snow. And everywhere, bullets whizzed in the air.

German soldiers in white winter uniforms ran from tree to tree, shooting in our direction. They were less than a hundred feet from us. I couldn't believe how close they were. As soon as they stepped from the cover of the trees to run toward our front lines, our machine gunners cut them down. But more and more kept coming, waves of them, and every one of them tried to shoot us dead before we could shoot them. The air was thick with lead.

I did not want to leave the foxhole. Why would anyone get out of a nice, safe hole in the ground to run around in the snow during a gunfight? As clearly as I could see the Germans running and falling, they would see me the moment I climbed out.

"Medic!" Another shout. "I'm hit! Medic!"

Goldsmith didn't turn around as he shouted at me: "Don't be a *yutz*! They need you. Get to work!"

Right.

Work.

I was a medic and someone was hurt. It was time to do my job. I hoped Goldsmith would be okay when I got back. I hoped I wouldn't be shot down the moment I raised my head. I hoped I wouldn't mess up before I could prove myself.

I took a deep breath, braced myself, and climbed out of my foxhole.

"Medic!"

"Medic!"

"Medic!"

I didn't know which way to go. Three different people had just shouted for a medic. I hesitated. I heard another slapping sound and then another loud whistle overhead.

"Incoming!" someone shouted.

I dove onto the ground, covering my head with my hands, as if that would stop the exploding shell from blowing me to bits. The shell hit a treetop above me. It burst into flames and a huge branch came crashing down. The branch landed just in front of me, and it was bigger than most trees where I grew up. I could smell the pine scent coming off of it, like Christmas.

Christmas was only a week away.

I really wanted to live that long.

I did not want to be on the ground anymore.

I stood and sprinted as fast as I could, keeping my head down, zigzagging so I wouldn't be an easy target for the Germans. The ground behind me burst as bullets snapped into the snow at my feet. I saw a foxhole ahead of me and I dove into it.

"Argh!" a guy grunted when I landed on him. "Medic!" he yelled.

"I am the medic!" I yelled back.

"Well, get offa me!" he grunted and shoved me off of him. I rolled over and looked at him. He was a guy about my age, with crystal-blue eyes and pale white skin. Like, really pale. I mean, most of the guys I'd seen in the army had lighter skin than me, but this guy was way too pale even for a white guy.

Something was wrong.

I looked down at his leg and I gasped. I had never seen anything like it before. He'd taken a piece of shrapnel from an artillery shell. The cloth was torn on his thigh, his tattered pant leg soaked through with bright-red blood. The blood had pooled at the bottom of the foxhole. He was almost bathing in it.

I recognized its color. In training we'd learned that if an artery was cut, the blood would be bright red, rich with oxygen, and under high pressure. It would squirt. The arteries carried the most blood through the body, and if they were cut, unless the bleeding could be stopped quickly, that kind of wound would kill a man. This soldier was in mortal danger. He was pale because he didn't have much blood left in his body. His wound squirted.

"How's it look, Doc?" he asked.

I'd never been called *Doc* before, although I knew that's what guys called the medics. It wasn't like I'd been to medical school or anything. I was just some guy who'd been assigned to be a medic the same way some guys were assigned to drive tanks. In my life before the army, I could no more treat a wound than drive a tank.

But now I'd been trained. I focused on my training, not on my fear, and I shoved my hand into the wound to try to get out the piece of shrapnel that had cut his artery.

"Ahh!" he screamed. I could only imagine how much it hurt.

"What's your name?" I asked, trying to distract him.

"Mike," he said.

"Hey, me too," I told him. "Miguel, but it's basically the same."

"Miguel, huh, you from — *ahh!*" he screamed again. My fingers dug around inside him, soaking my hand in that bright-red blood. I grasped a tiny piece of metal, so small it was hard to imagine it could do so much damage. I pulled it out and dropped it on the ground. Then I packed his wound with bandages and tied a cloth above the wound, tightening it to slow the bleeding.

"Medic!" I heard from another foxhole. "Medic!"

"Stretcher!" I called out, hoping someone would come to take Mike from the front lines. I'd stopped the bleeding, but if he didn't get to the aid station and get a blood transfusion soon, I feared he wouldn't survive.

"Medic!" The voice again. Desperate. Afraid. I was afraid too.

"Go," Mike said. "I'll be okay."

"You need to stay awake," I told him.

"Medic!"

"Go," Mike repeated.

"I'll be back to check on you," I said and exhaled, then lifted myself out of the foxhole and ran through the explosions and the gunfire of battle once more.

"Keep firing! Keep firing!" I saw a lieutenant running between the foxholes, just like I was, shouting encouragement to the soldiers, telling them where to aim, urging them to fight. He grabbed a grenade from his belt and flung it at an advancing German machine gunner, blasting the unfortunate German soldier to bits. The lieutenant glanced over at me, a proud expression on his face, like he'd just thrown the best fastball of his life. He still wore a smile a second later, when a bullet punched him in the chest and knocked him down.

I ran to him and dragged him behind a fallen tree for cover. The bark shattered over our heads as bullets sliced the tree to pulp, but it kept us safe.

"I'm okay," the lieutenant said, although he was not at all okay. "How old are you?" he asked me, studying my face.

"Eighteen, sir," I lied.

"Not a chance," he smirked. He saw right through me. "You even old enough to be a medic?"

"Yes, sir," I said. "Old enough to see you need one, sir."

He nodded and let me check his wounds. I opened his coat and found the bullet wound that had knocked him down. Then I found another. And another. And another. The blood seeped out of them, soaking into his uniform and mine. His breath wheezed and he coughed up thick red blood. The bullets had hit his lungs. I didn't even have time to press a bandage to his chest or give him morphine for the pain. He fell unconscious.

"Sir? Sir?" I shouted. He was our commanding officer. We needed him to tell us our orders, but instead, he died, just like that, right in my arms under a tree. He was only a few years older than me, maybe just out of college, and now he was gone.

It went like that for hours, wound after wound, frightened soldier after frightened soldier. Some were beyond my help and some just had minor scrapes and cuts. Their screams cut through the battlefield. They didn't cry out for their mothers. They cried out for their medic. They cried out for me.

"Medic! Medic!"

I needed to be in five places at the same time. I ran and jumped and dodged whizzing bullets. I must have gotten something on my boots from one of the injured men, because every step I took left a brownish-red footprint in the snow.

"Some morning, huh?" Goldsmith shouted at me. I hadn't even realized I was back in our foxhole.

I nodded. I couldn't find the words to speak. The guns did all the talking, while I tried to respond with bandages and painkillers and tourniquets.

"You okay?" Goldsmith asked me.

I nodded. "You?"

He nodded back, but he grinned too. "I was born for this," he said, and then he returned to shooting at Germans. "You like to pick on Jews!" he yelled at them as he fired. "I'll give you something to pick on. Pick on this!"

Pop. Pop. Pop.

"Medic!" I heard. Time to leave the foxhole again.

I no longer felt cold. I was too busy to be cold. There were more wounds than one medic could heal. There were gunshot wounds and burns, concussions and cuts and bruises and broken noses and smashed fingers. I found guys curled on the ground at the bottom of their foxholes, shaking and screaming and crying, and I couldn't find any kind of wounds on them. I did what I could for them, but I'd only been trained to fix their bodies. There wasn't anything I could do for their minds.

I scrambled out of one foxhole where a machine gunner had gotten some tiny metal fragments in his eye, and then ran to the next and slid down into it, catching my breath, trying to push away the horrible memory of the things I'd seen. Across from me, the sergeant who had dropped me off the night before sat with his back against the far side of the foxhole, his head tipped forward on his knees, napping. I didn't know his name and I didn't want to startle him awake. His helmet lay on the ground at his feet and I grabbed it to hand to him.

"Hey, Sarge?" I said quietly. Then louder, because if he could sleep through this battle, it would take some powerful noise to wake him up. "Sarge!" I yelled.

I tilted his head up to see what was wrong, but I stopped when I saw his face.

His eyes were wide open and just above them, his skull had been torn open. The bluish-red of his brains shimmered in the morning sunlight. I screamed and let him go. He slumped away from me into the mud at the bottom of the foxhole, beyond the help of any medic.

I shut my eyes and slid down to the bottom of the foxhole, and I started shaking. I had never seen so much horror, never even in my worst nightmares. How could so much have happened so quickly?

It was still morning, I thought, and I could hear the Germans shooting at us and our guys shooting back. German commandos in white snow camouflage came charging from the woods in waves and our big machine gunners cut them down and they fell just like tree branches into the snow. Mud and snow and blood all mixed together and the air smelled like metal and burning, a smell so thick you could taste it.

I sat there next to the dead sergeant and I just couldn't imagine climbing out of that hole again. I wasn't scared of getting killed. That thought didn't even occur to me. I simply didn't want to see anyone else hurt or anyone else dead. No more brains. No more blood. No more screaming. I didn't think I could bear it.

I don't know how long I sat there shaking. I heard voices far away, shouts between the explosions. When the loud thump of another artillery barrage came in, smashing the world around me to bits, shaking the earth underneath me, I curled up in the hole and shouted: "Enough! Enough!"

And then I started laughing, because I was shouting at artillery and it didn't make any sense at all. I was going nuts, I guess. No wonder the army hadn't given me a rifle.

I wished desperately then that they had. In that moment, I wanted nothing more than to remain in the foxhole, a gun at my side, firing into the Germans. I wanted to destroy them because of the fear they'd sparked in me. I was afraid and it was their fault and I wished so deeply to punish them for making me scared.

But I had no weapon. The best I could do was to help the riflemen fight by patching their wounds, undoing the terrible work of the German weapons. My revenge on the Germans would be in foiling their deadly designs.

I looked once more at the sergeant. I was too late to help him. I found myself annoyed instead of horrified, as if his dying were an insult to me and to my skill as a medic. He'd died in spite of me, almost like he was doing the Nazis a favor.

I would not do the Nazis any favors. I would not let them stop me from saving any more lives.

And yet, I didn't move.

My legs simply would not obey my new resolve.

I was scared.

It was my first battle, my first chance to prove myself. It was the whole reason I'd enlisted. And I was too scared to move.

Come on, Rivera, I told myself. *Don't be a coward. Get up. Get up, get up, get up.*

I was about to stand. I felt sure of it — just as an artillery shell smashed into the tree above the sergeant's foxhole. The great tree came crashing down above me. The branches crunched into the hole and blotted out the hazy sky. I put my arm up to protect myself, as if I could stop an entire tree from falling with just one arm, but it knocked me down beside the sergeant, and then my world went black.

DEVIL DOG

I woke in dimness. The pine smell filled my nostrils and I sat up, aching. My helmet was on the ground beside me. When I bent down to pick it up, my hand met the cold hand of the sergeant and I yelped. I scrambled out from beneath the fallen tree, sliding through the snow and the mud into the evening.

I must have been unconscious all day. The sun had set, and all around me was silence. The battle was over and I was alone.

A hot bolt of fear raced up my spine. It was like I'd woken up in a different place than where I'd fallen asleep. The ground was torn up, trees toppled, snow and mud and blood all mixed together into some kind of unholy stew. And the ground around the foxholes was littered with frozen bodies,

Americans and Germans, side by side, never to get up again. Through it all, I saw tank treads in the snow, passing right through.

The Germans had overrun our position. The Germans had overrun our position and I was alone behind enemy lines now and where were the rest of the Americans?

Where was Goldsmith?

I ran through the scarred landscape, tripping and falling over broken branches and jumping over obstacles at which I dared not look. I felt like I was in a nightmare. The foxhole that my friend and I had shared was empty. I jumped down into it, just to make sure, as if the small hole could hide anything.

"No, no, no," I muttered to myself, just to hear some sound in the graveyard silence of the battlefield. Worse than the chaos and terror of battle was the sinking feeling that I was totally alone. I was cut off from the rest of the American army by the German advance. I didn't really even know where I was. I needed to get back to friendly territory. I needed to find Goldsmith. I needed to —

I heard something.

There was a sound just above my foxhole — the crunching of snow — and then, a high-pitched whining.

I sucked in the chilly air and held my breath. I listened. Friend or foe? Was whining some kind of a code?

I peeked up from the foxhole and I saw a man lying on his back in the snow. He wore a heavy gray German officer's coat, and on his collar he had pinned two lightning bolts, the insignia of the Waffen-SS, the most feared of Hitler's soldiers. The whining seemed to come from him. He must have been in great pain to make such a noise, but his chest neither rose nor fell. There was no movement in him at all.

Still, however, he whined.

I lifted myself higher from the foxhole and the whining stopped. I didn't move. The man didn't move either. His eyes — wide open, lifeless — gazed up at the sky. I heard a growl.

I didn't know what to think. I had to ask myself: Could the dead growl?

And then, from behind him, a streak of black fur lunged at me, slobbering jowls and bright-white teeth. I fell back into the foxhole and held my arms up as a barking and snapping dog with raging eyes and wet, pink gums charged at me. The dog looked like the devil himself, come to collect my soul.

Just as the dog reached the top edge of the foxhole, it was

yanked back at the end of its own leash, its leather collar jerking it to a stop.

The dog scratched at the snow with its paws and barked down at me, straining to jump into my hole and tear me to shreds.

I had never a seen a dog like this before.

It was a big, barrel-chested creature, with black fur and a brown belly and snout. Its ears pointed up like devil horns from the sides of its narrow head. Beady black eyes fixed on me. I didn't know a lot about dogs, but I remembered seeing something in the paper about the Marine Corps using this same kind of dog, the Doberman pinscher. If US Marines used them, they must be fearsome.

"Easy, doggy, easy," I tried to calm it.

It stopped barking and cocked its head at me, curious. I stood slowly, my hands raised in the air, almost like I was surrendering. I kept my back pressed against the opposite side of the foxhole, as far away from that dog's jaws as I could be. It watched me stand.

"Good dog," I cooed. "Good devil doggy."

As soon as I went to climb out of the hole on the opposite side, the dog lunged again, barking like mad, and I slipped, sliding right back into the foxhole. The dog strained against its leash and inched forward. I saw that the leash was held by the SS officer, frozen in the dead man's hand. When the dog lunged, it dragged its master's whole body forward through the snow.

The dog had cut the distance between us in half and now towered over me in my foxhole, just out of reach. Every time I moved, it lunged, gaining a few inches each time.

I really needed to get out of this hole before more German soldiers came along. I did not want to be taken prisoner by a dog.

Or get eaten by one.

ALLIES

My teeth chattered so hard, I thought they might shatter. The forest was pitch-black. The moon hid itself behind the clouds, as if the war below was just too terrible to witness. I could hear the sound of gunfire in the distance, and the blast of more artillery. Someone somewhere was putting up a fight.

Not here, though. Here it was just me and the devil dog, and we'd both been tired out.

I leaned back against the far edge of the foxhole while the dog lay beside its master above me. Whenever I moved, it growled. When I stayed still, it stayed quiet. In the quiet I could hear vehicles in the distance and the pop of faraway gunfire. If the dog started barking again, it might just let the wrong people know I was here.

Listening above me, I heard the sound of the dog's tongue lapping at its master's frozen face, heard the unmistakable whine. I had never really liked dogs and definitely didn't like Nazis, but the sound of the dog whining for its master, who lay cold on the ground, filled me with sadness. It was like that whine said everything anyone needed to know about war.

I dared to lift my head up. The dog had his head resting on his dead master's chest. I admit: I felt bad for the mutt. But it was time for me to go find the Americans. I was cold and I was afraid, and I didn't want to die out here in the wilderness.

I made my move, pulling myself out of the foxhole as quickly as I could.

The moment my feet cleared the top of the hole, I rolled away so that the dog couldn't get me. He was up — the dog was definitely a *he* — and he rushed in my direction again, barking and slobbering. I saw the leash pull tight against his neck, lifting the frozen hand of the man on the ground as the dog dove at me. But he'd pulled too hard. Both the dog and his late master's body fell into the foxhole that I'd just escaped.

The dog landed with a yelp, followed by the thud of the body, and I thought maybe the one had crushed the other, but as I peered over, I immediately saw the dog start jumping and yipping, full of strength and power, still trying to get me.

"Give it up, you *yutz*," I told the dog, using Goldsmith's word for *fool*. "Don't you know when you're beat?"

But the dog didn't know. The dog kept at it. I was the enemy.

"Sorry, *vato*," I told it. "It's time for me to go."

I turned to walk away, then I heard the dog whimper. I peeked back and he had begun circling his master again, nudging him with his nose, whining and licking, trying to wake a man who would never wake again. But what could I do about it?

I shook my head and started off, following a row of boot prints in the snow. I hoped they were American boot prints. It would be a lucky break if I found the Americans before I ran into Germans. I hadn't been lucky so far, but I had to try. I still had my medical kit, so at least that was something. I was chilled to the bone and I wanted to lie down and sleep.

Even in the cold, my shame burned inside me. When the battle had started, I panicked. I couldn't get out of the fox-hole, and then, when I did, I got stuck. I failed to do my duty and I lost my unit. I'd come to be a hero and to defeat the Germans and I failed to do either.

But it wasn't my fault, was it? The tree had trapped me. The tree had knocked me out.

Why, then, did I feel like such a coward?

I stumbled along, berating myself like that for a while. On the one hand, I was a coward; on the other hand, it wasn't my fault. On the one hand, I had done my best; on the other hand, I knew that I had not done my best.

I hadn't made it far when I skittered down a steep embankment and landed in a puff of snow by the side of an icy road. I stood and brushed myself off and then I heard shouts, loud angry shouting . . . in German.

"Schnell! Schnell! Jetzt, los geht!" someone was yelling.

I ducked down behind the hedge and peered out at the road.

Heavy boots marched double time in my direction. Through the night fog, I saw shapes emerge, the shapes of men. First I saw German officers in their long coats and peaked caps, holding machine guns and trotting at the head of a column of soldiers. The soldiers were American. They were unarmed — some of them wounded, limping; others carrying the wounded. Germans flanked them on either side, yelling and shoving them. One of the Germans held a dog on a leash, a big German shepherd, even bigger and broader than the Doberman I'd left behind in the foxhole. The dog barked and snarled at the men.

They were prisoners, dozens of prisoners. I couldn't make out any faces, but I recognized the checkerboard shoulder patch some wore, just like my own. If Goldsmith was alive, this was where he'd be. They were being marched away from the front lines, toward Germany.

I listened as they passed, trying to stay silent. After a while, the sound of their marching faded. I stood. I didn't know what to do. I had to find the army, had to tell someone that the Germans had taken most of my unit prisoner. Maybe I could even tell them which way the prisoners were going. I could still redeem myself.

I pushed through the hedge onto the road, staying close to the ground where the fog was thickest, and I looked off in the direction they'd marched. It was too hazy to see anything. My heart sank. I didn't even know where I was, how could I tell anyone where they were going?

I sighed, disappointed in myself again. I'd panicked during the battle and lost my unit when it was taken prisoner, and now I'd been unable to help them even when I found them again. No wonder I had been assigned to be a medic. As a soldier, I was useless.

I turned and made my way back through the hedge, up the icy slope and through the snowy forest to the foxholes. I hoped perhaps I could find some other survivors, maybe an officer who could tell me what to do. As I trudged along, a light snow began to fall.

"Great," I muttered. "Just great." How was I supposed to find my way now? The fresh snow would cover up any existing footprints.

At least the snow would also cover all the blood.

When I reached my old foxhole, I didn't hear the dog anymore. I crept up carefully, on my hands and knees, freezing my fingers. I wasn't dressed for this kind of cold. I didn't even have gloves.

I looked into the hole and I saw the dog sound asleep beside his master, snoring. His legs twitched a little, like he was dreaming of the chase. Maybe he was dreaming about chasing American prisoners.

"Good riddance," I whispered, and turned to crawl around the hole, when my hand brushed something metal just at the edge of my foxhole. A chain.

I lifted it up from the snow. Dog tags. At the end of the

chain were the two thin plates of an American soldier's dog tags. I held them close to my eyes and saw whose they were:

Goldsmith, Albert. And there was his serial number and at the end of each tag, the letter *H* for *Hebrew.* My heart sped up in my chest. What did it mean that he'd left his dog tags here by the foxhole?

The chain was intact. These hadn't been torn off of him. He must have dropped the dog tags when the Germans overran the position, when he knew he'd be taken prisoner. Maybe he was afraid of what they'd do to him if they saw that he was Jewish.

We'd all heard the stories about Hitler and the Jews, about the terrible things he did. What would his army do to a Jewish soldier? The thought was too terrible to imagine. Maybe, if I had been there with him, I could have helped. Maybe we could have gotten away or hidden together.

Why should I have escaped when he didn't? He had saved my life. He had gotten me out of the foxhole to do my job. He was a better soldier than I was — braver too. And I had seen him march past, a prisoner, and all I had done was watch. I didn't even know which way they had gone. I had failed him. He was lost.

I sat down in the snow and stared at the sleeping dog and his master. Not that long ago, that dog had been with his unit, happy to serve, eager to tear apart any American he found. And then, the battle. And then, his master was killed. And still, he didn't give up. He tried to tear my throat out. And now, he just lay there, loyal to the end. He'd freeze to death or starve out here, probably, but he wouldn't give up. That dog was twice the soldier I was.

I stared at Goldsmith's dog tags. An idea came to me.

If that dog was twice the soldier I was, maybe I could use him! Maybe I could use him to track down the prisoners. He was a dog without a master. He'd want to go someplace familiar, like back to the Germans. If I could get him on that road, maybe he'd lead me after the prisoners, and then, maybe I could make up for my failure in the battle. Maybe I could find the prisoners and . . . well . . . I didn't know after that.

Rescue them? Or at least rescue Goldsmith. I had to save him before something terrible happened. I owed him my life, after all.

I nodded, feeling good about my decision. I stood up and stepped to the edge of the foxhole. I looked down on the dog and cleared my throat. He looked up at me, his devilish ears perked. I guess he was too tired to start barking again, which was a relief. But then he growled. Boy, did he growl.

"Don't growl at me, you *yutz*," I told him. "We need each other."

A BOY AND HIS DOG

The first thing I needed to do was get the dog to obey me. Or at least get him to stop trying to take my head off.

"What's your name?" I asked him even though I knew he couldn't answer me. I guess it just felt good to hear a voice, even if it was my own. All around the woods, it was dark, and I knew too well what lay beneath the thin layer of snow that had fallen. I did my best to focus on the dog in the foxhole, not the eerie lumps on the ground.

The dog cocked his head. His ears twitched and I saw his paws flex.

"Don't even think about jumping at me," I told the dog.

He growled at me again.

"Listen." I squatted down above the hole and looked

down at the dog. "I'll take you back to the Germans, but you gotta cut me some slack, okay?"

The dog barked. It was not a friendly bark. It was not an "okay, I understand and I'll help you find your friend" kind of bark. It was an intruder alert kind of bark, a "you are my enemy" kind of bark, the kind of bark that rang out through the forest, across the trees, and echoed off the silence of the snow. That kind of bark would call the Germans right to us.

"You're a real *yutz*, you know that?" I snapped at him. "I'm trying to help you."

If the dog wouldn't cooperate, I'd never get him out of that hole, and without him, I'd never find the prisoners. I'd have to retreat, try to avoid getting captured, and get back to the Americans, the only coward of the Ninety-Ninth to escape the battle. I wondered if they'd ask me questions, how I came to survive, why I was the only one. I didn't think I could bear to admit it.

But what was my other choice? To prove my courage by chasing down an entire SS unit to set their prisoners free . . . on my own? That wasn't bravery. It was madness. I was a brand-new army medic with one day of battle experience, not some sort of elite commando, trained to operate behind enemy lines. Retreat would not be cowardice. It was the only intelligent choice.

I looked at the tracks the German tanks had left, the deep gouges in the earth that were already filling with snow. If I followed them, they'd probably lead me right to the front lines. I'd be on the wrong side of the front, but maybe once I got there I could slip across unnoticed. The word *skulk* popped into my head, like a thief's skulk. I would skulk through the front and slink back to the army, my cowardice obvious to all.

I sighed and started walking.

"Erwww," I heard from behind me. The dog whining. I took another step away, my boots crunching the snow. "Erwww," again.

I looked back and the dog stood in the foxhole, his ears down, his stubby tail tucked. He lowered his head.

Maybe I would not have to skulk away after all.

"So now you want to play nice, eh?" I squatted above the foxhole. The dog whimpered.

I couldn't believe what I was about to do, but courage had to start somewhere. Why not with this dog?

I put my hand out.

The dog sniffed.

"Be a good boy," I said, trying to keep my voice calm and gentle. I needed the dog to stay relaxed.

I felt his cold, wet nose against my knuckles as he sniffed at me. I closed my eyes. I let him sniff. He didn't bite me, so I opened my eyes and eased myself forward.

"I'm coming down," I told him as I slid down into the foxhole. The dog backed away to the other side, but he didn't snap at me. "All right," I told him. "All right, now we're getting somewhere."

He watched me, his black eyes fixed on my every move as I bent down to look at his master. The man lay facedown now, one arm stretched in front of him and the other, the one where he held the leash, pinned beneath him against the hard earth. I'd have to roll him over to get the leash.

I really did not want to roll him over. I did not want to touch the body at all.

Okay, I thought. *You can do this. Just reach out and flip him over. It'll be fine.*

I squatted down and reached over the SS man. The dog growled.

"It's okay," I said. "I'm not going to hurt him."

I grabbed the man's coat. It was crusted with ice and

snow, but the fabric felt warm. I decided to take it from him. He wouldn't need it anymore and, well, I was so cold.

I started to pull it off him and the dog barked and lunged toward me. I held my arm up to protect my face, but the dog stopped before biting me.

"All right, all right," I said. "Let him keep the coat. It wouldn't have fit me anyway."

The German was a good six inches taller than me, and his shoulders were a lot broader. I grimaced as I reached down below him and found his ice-cold hand. As gently as I could, I pried the leash from his grip. When I pulled the leather strap out and held it in my palm, the dog sat. I guess he knew his job. I wished I knew how to speak a little German so I could give him commands, but we'd just have to learn to understand each other some other way.

I yanked the leash a little and the dog cocked his head at me again. He didn't move.

"We can't just stay here," I told him. "We've got a job to do. You see this guy?" I pointed at his master. "Where are the others? You're going to lead me to them, got it? *¿Comprende?*" I rolled my eyes; I couldn't believe I was talking to this dog. "Let's go. Out! Up!"

The dog didn't move. I stepped forward to grab him by the leather collar, but he growled a warning at me.

"Okay, okay. I'll keep my distance."

I didn't mind. He was a mean-looking dog, and keeping him a leash's length away suited me just fine. I didn't need him to be my best friend. I just needed him to lead me to the Germans and their prisoners without tearing my throat out. He stopped growling when I stepped back.

"We're going to have to leave your . . . uh . . . friend here," I said. "I'll go first."

I decided to climb out of the foxhole without looking away from the dog. I wasn't about to turn my back on him. He was still a Nazi dog and I was still an American soldier. But getting out while facing backward would take some shuffling and scrambling. At one point, I lost my grip and slipped back down into the hole again. The dog made a noise that I swear sounded like laughter. I tried again and managed to heave myself onto the ground, where I lay on my back for a moment, then stood and brushed myself off.

The snow fell harder now. The battlefield was covered in a white sheet and it looked almost serene. Nature had simply erased the horror of the battle that had occurred a few hours ago. The broken trees were the only evidence that anything unusual had happened here.

Of course, the snow meant that the footprints from the prisoners' march along the road would be gone too. I had to hope that the dog's instinct to find his masters would be strong enough to lead us. Part of me hoped that he couldn't. I silenced that voice inside my head, the coward's voice. I would not let it win.

I looked down at the dog and realized that, in my scrambling, I had dropped the leash.

"Great," I grumbled as I considered climbing back into the hole again. At least all this exercise kept me from freezing, or at least from feeling like I was freezing. "I don't suppose you know *come*, do you?" The dog scratched behind his ear with one of his powerful paws. I snapped my fingers. "Come! You *yutz*, I know you know what I want! Come!"

The dog gave a long look at the snow-covered German on the ground. He sniffed at him, and then he licked the dead man's face one more time, leaving a pale streak clear of snow along his cheek. Then, with a single thrust of his legs, he jumped from the foxhole and stood beside me.

I guess he understood that I was his new master now. Or at least he understood that he needed me until someone better came along. I felt the same about him. I picked up the leash.

"Come on." I yanked the leash in the direction of the road where I'd seen the prisoners, and the dog pulled me off my feet in the opposite direction. He basically dragged me over to one of the mounds in the snow and, to my horror, started digging.

"No! No!" I shouted at him. "Not there, you gigantic *yutz*!" The dog stopped digging and cocked his head at me. "I guess that's what I'll call you, huh? Yutz. Unless you can tell me a better name?"

The dog barked once, and pawed at the ground.

"Yutz, it is," I said. "What have you got there?"

I bent down and brushed the snow away from where the dog had been digging. I found what he was after: an open C-Ration, one of those disgusting cans of combat food that all US soldiers carried. The German attack must have come when some poor sap was trying to eat breakfast. He'd had just enough time to get the can open. It didn't look like he'd even taken a bite.

Yutz didn't wait for me to pull the can out of the snow. He lunged at it and shoved his face in, his whole snout, and he devoured the pasty meat substance. He was done in seconds and pulled his face out, licking his lips.

"Your first taste of American food?" I grunted.

I looked down at the lump in the snow. The dog wouldn't let me steal his dead master's coat, but he was happy to eat a dead American's food. He didn't even share. Dogs were supposed to be man's best friend.

This one was a jerk.

I decided that before going off after the prisoners the Germans had taken, I had better prepare myself for the mission. Yutz had sharp teeth and powerful jaws to fight with. I still just had my medic's bag filled with bandages and morphine and stuff. I bent down and dug into the snow pile for myself.

It was horrible, but I was looking for the fallen soldier's weapon.

I dug and I dug, but I didn't find it. I cleared more snow than I had wanted and I saw the dead soldier's face, looking up at me. It was an officer, another lieutenant.

"I'm sorry, sir," I said, and brushed his eyes closed. Then I kept searching his body for a gun.

The Germans must have taken it when they overran our position. As much as I didn't want to, I went to the next mound of snow and dug again. Again, no gun. The Germans must have taken them all. It seemed that this war did not want me to be armed with anything other than medicine.

It wasn't fair. I was all alone in a horrible wilderness, stuck with a Nazi dog who hated me and the corpses of a lot of men I never got the chance to know, while my only friend in the war, a guy who'd saved my life, had been hauled off into the night.

I'm not proud to admit it, but I cried. Right there, in the snow in the Ardennes forest, the Nazi dog watching me. I cried for a gun like a child cries for a lost toy, and my tears froze on the snow.

I wanted to go home. I wanted to run the other way, back toward the Americans, and never fight another day in my life.

But Goldsmith couldn't run away. None of the prisoners could. They were in danger, and I was the only one who knew which way they'd gone. I was the only one who had a dog that would follow them. I was the only one who could help. I was a medic, and it was my job to help.

Enough self-pity, I told myself. *You can be sad and scared later. Now you have to save your friends. And you have to make this dumb German dog help you do it.*

"Okay, Yutz." I pushed myself off the ground and wiped my face. "You ready to save my friends, you stupid mutt?"

The dog sat down and licked himself, ignoring me completely.

"No way, *vato*," I said, snapping his leash. "We're going to find my friends."

He snorted and slobbered at me, shook the snow from his fur, and lifted a paw while he sniffed the air.

"This way," I told him and tugged him back in the direction that I wanted to go. This time, he obeyed.

Or maybe it was the way he wanted to go after all, because the moment we scrambled down the hill behind the hedge, he sniffed the air and dragged me out onto the road. There were tank treads and jeep tracks frozen in the road, although the snow had mostly buried them. The footprints were already gone.

"Okay, Yutz, find your masters. Go!"

He didn't even look at me. He just stopped, right in the middle of the road, and sniffed up at the breeze. I glanced back, worried more Germans would be coming along, but the wind howled and swirls of snow cut off visibility. I couldn't see ten feet in front of me or behind, which meant that Germans coming this way couldn't either. But in this case, I had an advantage. I had a dog who wanted to go home.

Yutz pulled me along in the direction I had seen the column of prisoners going, and I hoped it was their smell he was following. I held on to that leash and did my best to keep up, although I kept stumbling. The first time I fell, Yutz yelped with the surprise of being yanked backward by the neck. The second time, he growled at me. By the fifth or sixth fall, he just stopped and waited until I got up again, and I swear I heard the wheezy dog-laughing sound. Once I was on my feet, he lunged forward again, and I stumbled after.

"Slow down, Yutz," I said. "I'm not used to all this ice."

I remembered what Goldsmith had said: "No snow in the desert."

I'd lost hours coaxing the dog away from that foxhole, and now he was my only chance to find them again. He was my chance at redemption. I could still be a hero. No one had to know that I'd panicked during the battle. That would be my private shame. All anyone would need to know was that I had escaped capture to rescue my friends.

I focused hard on every step as I ran behind the dog, clinging to the leash, determined not to fall.

The howling wind sounded like a pack of dogs chasing us through the night.

WILDHUND

I followed the Doberman for the rest of the night, his black-and-brown fur almost invisible in the dark.

On the ground, the road was empty. I started to wonder if we were even going the right way, but then I saw a man lying facedown on the ground by the side of the road. He had a dusting of snow over him, and as Yutz dragged me closer, I saw that he wore an American uniform. He'd died on the march and the Nazis had left his body unburied in a ditch. I pulled Yutz back and we went on. I couldn't save him, whoever he was. I didn't have time to bury the dead. I barely had time to help the living.

As we went down the road, I saw two more bodies. I approached each of them, heart pounding in my chest, and bent down to see their faces. I didn't know them. They weren't Goldsmith. We kept going.

As we rounded a bend in the road, the dog stopped. He lifted one of his front legs and perked his ears. They twitched on the top of his head.

"What is it?" I asked him. I didn't know what his sudden alertness meant. Was someone coming? Should we hide?

Then I saw his nub of a tail wag, and he barked, pulling me forward. I followed. It was the first time I'd seen his tail wag. He must have smelled something he liked, and the sight of his tail wagging made me hopeful.

Until I remembered that what he liked was German soldiers! I'd forgotten that Yutz and I were not on the same side.

I dug my heels into the ice and pulled back hard on the leash, so hard that the dog slipped and lost his footing, sliding down onto the snow with a sudden yelp.

"Wer is da?" a voice yelled through the fog. *"Zeigen Sie sich! Hände hoch!"*

I didn't speak German, but I sure knew what it sounded like. The dog tried to get up and run toward the man, but I heaved him in the other direction. He fought me every step of the way, and he started barking like mad. He was ninety pounds of pure muscle, and I couldn't pull him across the ice.

"Zeigen Sie sich!" the German in the fog shouted again. I still couldn't see anyone. I hoped that meant he couldn't see me either.

I had to think quickly. I could let the dog go and hide on my own, give up on using him to find the prisoners. He might just as soon turn around and lead the Germans right to me, though. He knew my smell now. I didn't know if dogs could do that, but I figured they could. That's why police used dogs to track escaped convicts and why hunters used dogs to catch animals. Was that a special kind of dog? Was Yutz one of those? I had no idea. I didn't want to take the chance.

I yanked the leash again so he lost his footing, and at the same time I rushed around to his side. I decided that I couldn't charge straight at him or he'd just bite me, so I dove at his big black flank and landed on top of him with a thump. He struggled and squirmed under me, snarling loudly and trying to turn his head and bite my arm. He was better at wriggling than I was at wrestling, and I was about to lose my grip on him.

"Jetzt! Zeigen Sie sich!" the voice yelled once more. He sounded frightened. The last thing I needed was to be discovered by a frightened German with a gun.

As I struggled to hold Yutz down, I looped the leather leash around his long brown snout, once, twice, three times, pulling tight, muzzling him. He stopped struggling. He looked up at me with his dark dog eyes and he flattened his ears. I figured he'd given up the fight, at least for now, and I jumped off him, holding the leash-muzzle tight, no slack at all. Then I dragged him to the side of the road. He followed, his whole rear end low to the ground and his feet skittering on the ice. He was going with me, but he wasn't helping. When we got to a ditch, I pulled him down and crouched over him so that I could see and so that he was secure underneath me. That way, he couldn't make a break for it.

"Ist jemand da?" I saw a form emerge from the fog. The German held a rifle out in front of him, and pivoted from side to side, surveying the road. He drew closer and closer to our hiding spot. The dog beneath me didn't wriggle, and thanks to the muzzle, he couldn't bark, but I heard him let out a low whimper, a longing to answer the only language he'd ever known.

I wasn't cruel. I felt for the dog. It wasn't his fault he'd been born in Germany at a time when dogs like him were trained and turned into Nazi soldiers. It wasn't his fault his master had died or that I'd found him. But none of that mattered. I didn't want to be here any more than he did, but I couldn't let myself fall back into self-pity, and I wasn't about to let the dog do it either.

"Shh, Yutz," I whispered right into his ear, and he stopped whimpering. His eyes rolled up to look at me and he flattened his ears against his head. I guess he'd accepted our relationship: He was my prisoner.

As the soldier walked by our hiding spot in the ditch, I could finally see him clearly. He was young, younger even than I was, maybe fourteen or fifteen years old. His cheeks were bright red with the cold and his hand shook on the rifle stock. His coat was far too large for him, his helmet too. It slumped down over his whole forehead and partway over his eyes. It was a wonder he could see anything at all.

"Wer is da?" the boy soldier said again. I could see his breath in the air in front of him, puffing out like steam from a train engine, his breathing was so fast. He was even more afraid than I was. His gun turned and pointed at every noise. We were so close I could see his finger twitching on the

trigger. I feared that so much as a sigh from the dog would make the young man open fire. I feared that even my heart was beating too loudly.

After the longest minute of my life, the soldier backed away in the direction he'd come.

"War nur ein Wildhund," he said to someone. I didn't want to stick around to find out what that meant. I eased up off of Yutz and gave his leash a tug. We crept along the ditch by the side of the road, slipping behind a ring of sandbags where the boy and another young soldier crouched with their rifles, pointing them at the road. I held Yutz on a very short leash, and whenever he left my heel, I gave it another tug. He looked up at me resentfully, but obeyed. We made it past the soldiers unseen and moved along as quickly as we could, although I was more careful to keep to the side now, and we moved a little more slowly. I did not want any more surprise meetings with nervous young Germans and their nervous trigger fingers.

We encountered no one else as we went along, and after a while, I let Yutz have a longer leash. I unwound his muzzle so that only one loop held his mouth closed, and I even let that hang slightly loose so that he could pant more freely. He was my prisoner, but that didn't mean I had to make him suffer. I hoped the German soldiers were giving the same consideration to their prisoners.

When we reached the edge of a town, I was dismayed to discover that they were not treating their prisoners even half as well I was treating mine.

A TOWN IN MORNING

The town looked like nothing I had ever seen before. The sun had started to rise, but with the heavy cloud cover and the continued snow, everything was cast in a soupy gray — lighter, but somehow not brighter. I hid in a row of trees on a hill at the edge of the town, from which I could see down into the central square — or rather, I could see the ruins of the central square.

There was a church, its steeple blasted clean off. The old stone buildings all around it were either totally collapsed or so riddled with bullet holes that they looked like they were made of lace, not stone. Rubble blocked the streets — and not just rubble. Amid the crumbled stones and wooden fragments, there were possessions, tossed from the houses by whatever explosive force had leveled this town. I saw a smashed piano flipped onto its back, a burned car crushed beneath the wall of a house, rags and broken plates, heaps of ruined chairs and tables, smashed picture frames, and the crushed body of child's toy rocking horse.

And then I saw the people.

There were about fifteen of them clustered around a small fire by the side of the church. They were dressed in mismatched layers of clothes, bundled against the cold in whatever they could find. There were a few old women and a few old men and three or four small children. No young adults, no teenagers or men of fighting age. They stood close together but didn't speak, looking down at the ground or into the fire, their faces thin and tired.

When I had passed through France on my way to the front line, the only civilians I had seen waved flags at our trucks. They cheered and danced in the streets as we went by. We had liberated them from the Nazis, and they treated us like heroes before we'd even gotten to the front lines.

These people were not liberated. Their town had been the scene of a fight, and was under Nazi control now. From the looks of it, no matter who won the battle raging across Belgium, this place had already lost. These bedraggled people were all that was left.

I heard a shout and one of the old men looked up. I followed his gaze to the rear corner of the church and saw a Nazi officer step into view, dressed in the familiar long coat and peaked cap. Even from my distance, I could make out the shine of the two lightning bolts on his collar, the SS.

The SS weren't like normal German Army soldiers. They were a special organization, run by the Nazi leadership, not the German Army, and they were the only ones Hitler trusted. The SS were the ones who murdered civilians, burned entire villages. They were the ones who rounded up the Jews of Eastern Europe to slaughter them like cattle. From everything I'd heard, the German Army guys were basically all right, just normal soldiers that fought hard, but knew when they were beat. The SS, on the other hand, had this idea of "resistance to the death." They were the ones who would rather see the whole world burn than surrender.

And they were the ones who had taken my friend.

The SS officer beckoned for the old man at the fire to come to him. I watched as the officer asked the old man some sort of question. When he was satisfied, the officer pointed to the side of the church I couldn't see, and from around the corner came two more German soldiers, normal army men in army coats and helmets, not the feared SS.

Behind them marched an American with his arm in a sling and behind him another, limping, and then another and another and another. They marched silently, single file, ten, twenty, thirty, forty, fifty, and more. I lost count. They just kept coming, and the old man led them to the small fire, where they huddled together, far too many men for too small a fire. The civilians scattered, disappearing into the dark doorways of the ruined buildings.

I didn't see them again.

I noticed that most of the Americans didn't have shoes on. They marched across the freezing, snowy ground in their green army socks, some of which were already mere shreds so the men were barefoot in the snow. Toward the back of the line, hobbling along with his helmet still perched on his head, I saw Goldsmith, looking down at the ground, trying to avoid drawing any attention to himself. A man behind him limped and used Goldsmith's shoulder for balance.

Relief came over me like a warm blanket. My friend was alive. He was walking, and although his feet must have been in pain, he did not appear gravely injured.

At the back of the line of Americans, there were a few more German Army soldiers, and three more SS men, surveying the huddled crowd of prisoners. One of them led the big brown-and-black German shepherd I had seen the previous night. The dog looked alert, his eyes fixed on the American soldiers trying to warm their hands and feet around the fire. Beside me, through his muzzle, Yutz whined.

"Friend of yours?" I asked. I could feel him straining on the leash, every muscle in his body wanting to run to the dog and its master.

"Funf minuten!" the SS officer yelled at the Americans.

Suddenly, a small blond boy ran out from the shadows of a mostly destroyed house and rushed up to the Americans. He had curly golden hair that shined in the dim morning light like a halo or a crown. It was the only vivid color in the otherwise gray-and-brown landscape.

He approached the injured man beside Goldsmith and tugged his tattered pants. The man turned down to the boy and I saw the soldier's face. It was Mike, the guy whose bleeding shrapnel wound I'd treated, my first act as a battlefield medic. He leaned on Goldsmith for support, but he had some color back in his face. I was glad to see him alive, glad to see he was on his feet. It looked like I wasn't such a bad medic after all.

The boy shoved something into Mike's hand and ran off again. The SS men watched him go, but said nothing.

Mike whispered something to Goldsmith and tore off a piece of what the boy had given him.

Bread. It was bread. He offered some to Goldsmith.

I couldn't tell what my friend said, but his gestures were clear enough. He turned it down, pushed the piece back to Mike. I guess he figured the injured man needed it more. I suppose he was right. But Mike insisted, even after Goldsmith refused again, so he ate a little bit and then passed his chunk of bread down the line for a few others to get a taste.

My stomach growled.

Goldsmith was a better man than I. I think I would have eaten that whole chunk without even chewing. For a second, I considered surrendering, just to get something to eat.

The Germans laughed at something and then they started shouting, pulling the prisoners away from the fire and making them stand in line with their backs to the church wall.

Icy fear gripped me. It looked like they were being lined up in front of a firing squad.

I had to do something. I had to think of a plan, fast. All the German soldiers were armed with machine guns, and there was that ferocious dog down there. Plus the one up here that I still couldn't trust. If I let him go, he'd turn on me, and I'd have a whole squad of Nazis plus two trained-killer dogs to deal with.

While my mind raced with ideas, each one worse than the last, the SS officer started speaking. He didn't order his men to fire. It wasn't that kind of line the Americans were in. The officer spoke to them in English.

"American invaders!" he shouted, his accent crisp and sharp. "I am Obersturmführer Schultz and you are prisoners of the German Reich. You will be treated justly if you obey our commands. If you disobey, if you attempt sabotage or if you attempt escape, you will be shot."

Obersturmführer was a rank like first lieutenant in the US Army. Schultz was the commander of this group, and it looked like he made the regular German Army guys nervous.

"We will continue our march in three groups!" he shouted. "Officers, you will stand here."

He pointed, and there was a murmuring and a shuffling of feet among the Americans. I saw some lieutenants, two captains, and even a major step to the spot where they had been commanded to stand.

"Enlisted men!" Obersturmführer Schultz shouted at the rest of them. "You will be in two groups. All American soldiers who are Jews, step forward!"

No one moved.

"Do not be alarmed," the SS officer said. "It is for your own protection."

Still, no one moved. My heart thumped in my chest. Why was he singling out just the Jewish soldiers?

Goldsmith stood still. He let Mike lean on him and he did not step forward.

"If you continue to disobey," Obersturmführer Schultz said calmly, "you will be shot."

"You can't do that!" the American major yelled. "These men are prisoners of war and under the laws of war, you cannot simply begin —"

One of the other SS men hit the major in the back with the end of his rifle, knocking him into the snow.

"I repeat," Schultz snapped. "Jewish soldiers, step forward."

The SS dog handler made a noise and the big German shepherd barked.

A guy I didn't know took a hesitant step forward. He made no eye contact with anyone else. Everyone tensed.

"Nur eine?" Schultz grumbled. "Only one? I think not."

He began to walk along the line of Americans, looking each one up and down, holding his Luger pistol in his hand. The SS dog handler followed him. Every few men, Schultz would nod, the dog handler would grunt and the American would be pulled out of line to stand with the Jewish soldiers.

"But I'm not a Jew," one of them objected. He was a short Italian-American private that I recognized from boot camp. Sebastiano Campisi. Like Goldsmith, he was from New York, but I guess they didn't know each other. Goldsmith stood rigid, looking straight ahead.

The officer ignored Private Campisi's objections.

"We need thirty volunteers," he said. "If there are no more Jews, others will be chosen."

He continued down the line, getting closer and closer to Goldsmith, who stared down at his socks in the snow. The officer walked past him. I let out a sigh of relief, but perhaps it was too soon.

Schultz stopped a few feet farther on.

He turned back and walked up to Goldsmith, lifted Goldsmith's chin with his index finger and looked him in the eyes. He nodded and my friend was pulled roughly from the line. Mike held on to him for support.

"Let go," Schultz commanded. Some of the other Americans grabbed Mike and held him up as Goldsmith was pulled forward. "You should have volunteered," the officer sneered at Goldsmith. Then he raised his pistol. Goldsmith closed his eyes. So did I.

A shot rang out.

I opened my eyes and saw Mike, the man whose life I had saved, the only one I could be sure I'd saved, lying in the snow, a red stain spreading out beneath his head like spilled paint. He didn't move.

The others immediately started shouting and pressing forward toward the murderer, but the big dog barked and one of the German Army guys fired his machine gun into the air.

"Disobedience will be punished!" Schultz yelled. The lightning bolts on his collar gleamed even in the dim light of the overcast morning. "You are responsible for one another's actions. I trust that lesson has now been understood!"

He grunted some more commands at his men, and the German Army guys began marching the American officers and the enlisted men in a long line back to the road, leaving the town for the long march into Germany. The SS men stayed with Goldsmith and the other soldiers who had been pulled out of line.

"You are going to a very special place," I could hear Schultz telling them. The snow and the stillness of the air made the sound travel so clearly, it was like he was whispering in my ear. A chill ran up my spine. "Do not dream of running away. Even if you escape, the others who remain will pay the price. Now!" he yelled. *"Los! Geht!"*

Goldsmith and the others looked at one another, confused. Even though they probably understood that the officer wanted them to start marching, they weren't about to make it easy for him to drag them away. Sort of like Yutz, I guessed. Sometimes, even when you know you have to obey, you resist in little ways just to know that you can. Resisting like that might not destroy your enemies, but it will keep them from destroying you.

"Go!" the officer shouted and started shoving the men forward, toward a different road than the rest of the Americans had taken out of town.

They began moving very slowly, dragging their feet.

"Keep it up," I whispered. "Just keep going slow until I can save you."

As they moved out, the SS dog handler took up the rear of the line. His big dog barked and the men sped up their pace a little.

The bark must have set something off in Yutz, because he snapped his head suddenly to the side, slipping right out of the loop of his leash that had muzzled him, and he let out a loud series of barks. They cut the morning air as loud as machine-gun fire and they were, to me, just as deadly.

I pressed myself down flat on top of him, pushing his face against the snow, and I rewrapped the leather strap around his snout three times and yanked it tight, probably harder than I should have, but it silenced him. Yutz relaxed again, having gotten out his message.

It was probably a call for help.

My breath came fast now, puffing out in frosty blasts. I dared lift my head again to look, and I saw that the handler and his dog had broken from the back of the line. They were walking across the square, heading straight for the other side of town — the side where I was hiding.

The dog led his master with his nose in the air, sniffing, searching for the scent of the dog that had barked, the dog lying calmly beneath me.

I could swear that underneath his muzzle, Yutz had a cruel doggy smirk on his face.

We had to hide.

THE BARN

I dragged Yutz behind me, scrambling through the snow toward a barn about thirty yards away. Yutz resisted, planting his back legs and leaning away from me. I had to use both hands to pull him along.

I realized too late that the dog handler wouldn't even need to use his German shepherd's keen nose to find us. We were leaving an obvious trail of footprints — boots and paws — and big, long drag marks where Yutz made me pull him. There wasn't time to do anything about it. I couldn't see the SS dog team anymore, but I knew they'd be coming over the top of that hill any second now, and we were totally out in the open. All I could think about was getting inside that barn.

Once we were inside, I shut the door and dragged Yutz to a stall in the back. There was a slight scattering of hay, but otherwise the barn was empty. All the animals gone. I pulled Yutz down and held him tightly in my arms so he couldn't wiggle free or make any more loud noises. He squirmed at first, but finally he relented.

His chest rose and fell with rapid breaths, and his nostrils flared at the end of his nose. I could feel his heart beating against my hands, but with every second that passed, he relaxed a little more. I guessed that even for a war dog, it felt good to be held. It felt safe. I had to admit, holding him against me, I felt a little safer too. I knew the dog wasn't on my side, but he was warm and soft and he made me think of home.

Any good feeling I had in that cold damp barn vanished when the door creaked open and I heard the clomp of heavy boots and the panting of a large dog. The SS dog handler had stepped inside.

"Hände Hoch! Zeigen Sie sich!" he commanded. Yutz squirmed in my arms. I didn't understand German, but he did. Every part of his body screamed out for escape. Freedom was so close, he could smell it. I squeezed him tighter. His freedom would mean the end of mine.

I heard the footsteps coming closer. The big dog snorted loudly. Yutz whimpered and the tiny noise sounded like a thunderclap to me. I held my breath. Yutz whimpered again. The German shepherd barked and I could feel Yutz's chest heave, trying to let out a bark in response.

"Hände Hoch!" the dog handler repeated slowly, very quietly, and I knew the game was up. Maybe if I surrendered, he wouldn't let his dog attack me. I looked down at Yutz's frantic eyes. Yutz would have loved to make a chew toy out of my head if he had the chance. I began to slip Yutz off my lap, letting go with one hand, while I held the leash with the other so that I could stand.

Just as I started to move, I saw a glimmer in the barn stall across from me, a golden ring in an ash heap. It took me a moment to realize it was the little boy who had brought the Americans that piece of bread. He slid out of the shadows and met my eyes. He put his finger to his lips, urging me to be quiet, and then he made a whimpering noise that sounded almost exactly like Yutz's. He stepped to the center of the barn with his hands raised above his head, shuffling toward the SS soldier and his big Nazi dog.

"*Nicht schiessen*," he whimpered. That was a German phrase I knew. We had all learned it on the boat heading over to Europe. It meant "don't shoot."

I felt like a coward. There I was, lying on the floor of a barn, clutching a dog to my chest while a little boy risked his life to protect me. Some soldier I was.

But still, I stayed down and did my best to keep Yutz quiet.

The dog handler grunted some questions at the boy, and the boy answered them in tearful whispers. Then the man yelled, and his big dog barked again.

The boy yelped.

The dog handler said something else. I didn't know what it was, but the tone was clear. It was the same tone adults all over the world used when they scolded children.

The boy answered in the same tone boys all over the world use when they apologize for whatever they've been scolded for, even if they didn't do it.

I heard the horrible click of a pistol being cocked. The Nazi dog handler shouted, but a loud whistle cut the air. Obersturmführer Schultz was calling his dog handler back. The other SS men probably didn't want to stand around waiting for this guy and his dog anymore. The dog handler exhaled loudly and shouted something in return.

I pictured Schultz, who had shot Mike in cold blood, checking his watch and tapping his foot impatiently on the snow, like a coach when his team was late for baseball practice. I held my breath. Would this man shoot this boy dead before returning to his unit?

The boy didn't make a sound. Neither did I. I heard the clomp of heavy boots and the creak of the barn door. The dog's paws crunched the snow as he followed his master down toward the village.

Yutz lay on my lap, his nostrils flaring with deep breaths, like he was trying to inhale the Nazi and his dog, breathing them back to rescue him from his American captor: me.

But they were gone, and I hoped that when their smell faded, so would Yutz's agitation. His barking had nearly gotten me captured, and I wondered now if trying to use him to track the prisoners would be more trouble than it was worth.

"American?" The little boy startled me, standing at the end of the barn stall, looking at me and Yutz with curiosity. His voice was stronger and clearer than I'd expected from how he had whimpered. He stood taller too, not nearly so small as he'd seemed with the Germans around. He must have been eleven or twelve years old.

I thought about myself when I was that age, running around the hard-baked earth outside my grandmother's house, while she shouted at the kids to come in for dinner, waving her big rice spoon in the air. The thought made me smile. *Oh,* Abuela, *if you could only see me now,* I thought, *almost eighteen, a soldier, cowering in fear while a tiny boy stands up to the Nazi SS.* This was not my proudest moment.

I nodded and let Yutz slide off my lap as I stood slowly, keeping his leash and the loops around his mouth pulled tight. He growled at the boy, but the boy did not back away. He just cocked his head at the dog and Yutz stopped growling. He mirrored the boy, cocking his head too. For a moment they stood like that, puzzled mirrors of each other, while I stood in my dirty uniform, towering over both of them, yet feeling like the smallest thing in the whole barn.

Yutz started to growl again, but the boy growled back and the dog flatted his ears against his head.

The boy shrugged and looked back up at me.

"Hugo," he said, which I figured was his name. Then he saluted me.

"Miguel," I said and saluted him back.

"Meeguile?" the boy repeated, his accent thick.

"Close enough," I said.

We stood staring at each other for a while. Then I had an idea. I rummaged in my medic's supply bag for a second and found a foil-wrapped chocolate bar. I pulled it out and tossed it to him.

"Chocolat?" He smiled as he unwrapped it.

I nodded and he bit into it with a satisfying snap as the cold chocolate broke into his mouth. He took two bites and then offered it back to me. In truth, I was hungry, but, thinking of Goldsmith, I held my hand up and refused. Hugo wrapped the chocolate up and put it in his pocket.

"You wait," he said to me. "Here. No problem. You wait."

Then he ran out of the barn, leaving me and Yutz alone again. Yutz looked up at me, his dog eyebrows raised.

"I don't know either," I told him. Yutz growled at me. "What's the kid got that I don't?"

Yutz just looked away. He lay down, resting his head on his paws. His pointy ears twitched.

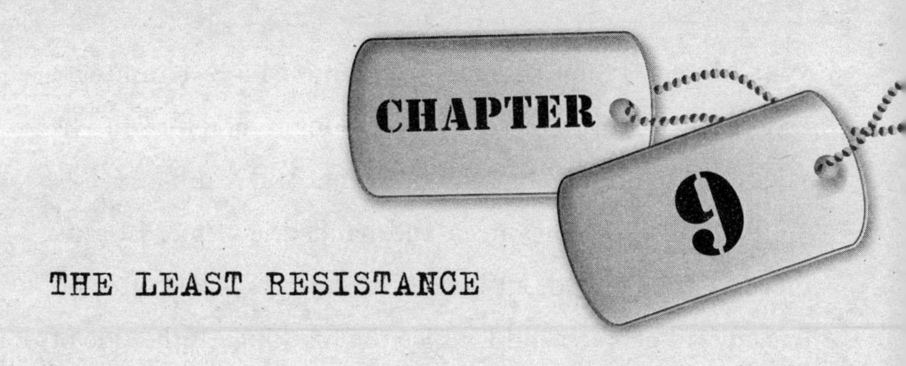

THE LEAST RESISTANCE

A few minutes later, the barn door creaked open again. I ducked behind the stall and Yutz sat up, turning his nose and ears to the door. He didn't bark.

"Meeguile?" the boy called.

I stepped out into the open. Hugo had returned, but he wasn't alone. A man was with him, a thin man with a shaved head and a scraggly blond beard. His eyes were blue just like Hugo's.

"My papa," Hugo said, and the man stepped forward. He shook my hand.

"Michel," he said.

"Miguel," I corrected him.

"No, no," the man laughed. "My name is Michel. Like

your Miguel. From Michael. The same name." He slung a canvas bag off his shoulder. "I have brought food for you," he said. "It is not much, but you must eat. And drink."

He pulled out a canteen and handed it to me. I drank greedily as he pulled out bread and sausages. Only after I'd had my fill of water did I notice the marking on the side of the canteen: the swastika, symbol of the Nazis.

"The spoils of war, yes?" the man explained. "Taken from the Germans."

He reached back into his bag and pulled out a heavy gray Nazi SS officer's coat and handed it to me.

"You will move better in this," he said. "If you are seen it is less likely you will be stopped."

"You've done this before, huh?" I asked him.

He smiled. *"La Resistance,"* he said. "The Resistance. We have helped many Americans to escape. We will help you."

"I'm not trying to escape," I told him. "I want to help my friends who were taken prisoner."

Michel ran his fingers through his beard. "The prisoners . . . This is not easy. They have been separated."

"I need to help the smaller group," I told him.

"The officers?"

"No, the other group."

"The Jews." He sighed. "The Undesirables, as they call them."

"Undesirables?" I asked. I didn't like the sound of that.

"The Nazis believe they are the master race," Michel said. "They believe that anyone who is not like them is inferior, undesirable. So they take the Jews they capture, and anyone who they think looks like a Jew, and they send them to work camps in Germany. Very bad places. Many die there. Belgian, German, Polish . . . even British and American. They are called work camps, but they are truly camps for dying. They are death camps."

"I can't let them take my friend there," I said.

"The SS will take these prisoners to the train depot," Michel said. "A train will take them into Germany, to the camps."

"Then I have to get them before they reach the train depot," I told him.

"The march will take them some days," Michel said. "All their fuel and equipment goes in the other direction, on the attack."

"Yeah," I grunted. "I noticed the attack."

"The Americans have been pushed back, no? You think the Germans will prevail?"

"Not a chance," I said.

"The SS will not allow their prisoners to escape so easily," said Michel. "You will need help."

"From you?"

"I am needed elsewhere. It is the German attack that concerns me." Michel thought for a moment. "Hugo can take you to find some other Americans. We know where they are."

"Hugo?" I wrinkled my forehead to show my objection. "He's too young."

"As are you, my friend," Michel said gravely. "But we all do our part to fight the Nazis. And Hugo knows the countryside well."

"But the Germans are getting away. If I detour for help, I'll lose their trail."

"Following my son, you will not lose much time. And this dog can help you find the trail again."

I looked at Yutz. He did not seem eager to help me.

Michel asked, "Why do you have this dog?"

"The spoils of war," I told him.

He laughed. "The Germans train their dogs very well. They train them to find escaped prisoners, train them to stand guard, and train them to attack the enemy. I have even heard Hitler tries to train dogs to speak in code and to read messages . . ." The man shook his head and laughed. "Though Hitler is mad, this last part I do not believe."

"Me neither," I said, looking at Yutz, picturing the big black Doberman with bifocals and a newspaper spread out before him. I had to laugh.

While I spoke to his father, Hugo had knelt in front of Yutz, close to the dog's big snout. He was turning his head side to side, looking at the dog from different angles. The dog kept turning to avoid direct eye contact with the boy. Even with his leash wrapped around his snout, I worried about the child being so close to the mean dog, but he wasn't afraid at all.

In fact, Yutz seemed afraid of the boy.

"If you can control him, he could be of valuable help to you," Michel said.

"I think he hates Americans," I told Michel.

"Dogs are not like people," Michel said. "They do not hate."

"Well, he sure doesn't like me very much."

"You must give him a reason to like you," Michel said. "Give him some water." He held out the canteen to me again.

"Water?"

"A thirsty animal cannot resist water," Michel said. "And all friendships must begin somewhere."

I guessed Michel was right. I hadn't given Yutz any reason to like me. All I'd done was tackle him and wrap his snout and drag him away from his master. Then again, he'd tried to get me killed or captured, so it only seemed fair.

I sighed and pulled him over to one of the posts at the end of the stall. I unlooped the leash from around his snout and I tied the leash to the post. Yutz didn't bark or snarl when I let his mouth go. He yawned, showing his big white fangs and his long pink tongue, then he spun in a circle and curled into a tight ball, with his head resting over his front paws. I guess even ferocious Nazi war dogs got tired.

I took the canteen from Michel and bent down in front of the doubtful-looking dog. He met my eyes and growled a low belly-growl.

"You aren't thirsty?" I asked him.

Hugo and his father stood behind me, watching. I could feel their eyes on the back of my neck. I felt ridiculous, kneeling in front of a big black war dog, begging him to take a drink.

Yutz studied me, studied my outstretched hand. He lifted his head and sniffed at the air, stretched a little farther, and sniffed the opening of the canteen. I tilted it and let a little drop of water pour out. Yutz snatched it from the air with his tongue. I poured a little more and Yutz opened his mouth, lapping it in, gulping it. When he'd had his fill, he sneezed once, blasting excess water through his nose, and then he looked up at me. He laid his head back down onto his paws.

He didn't bark or growl. A moment later, he snored.

I guess ignoring me for a nap was a kind of progress.

I wondered how he would feel when I woke him up again. We had to go get help and save the prisoners from a Nazi death camp. There was no time for naps.

TOPPLED SNOWMEN

I ate some of the bread and sausage that Michel had brought me and then I put on the heavy SS coat right over my army uniform. It was much warmer than my thin army jacket. I might've looked a little puffy with all those layers, but it was better than freezing to death.

Hugo wore only thin pants and a light coat. He covered his head with a green wool cap, hiding his brilliant blond hair beneath it. Even though it was freezing out, his teeth didn't so much as chatter. There was a toughness to him I couldn't begin to imagine. I hoped some of it would rub off on me.

While I buttoned up the gray SS coat, Michel knelt down and whispered something to his son in French. The boy nodded and wiped a tear from his father's cheek. Michel hugged him close, pressing his face into his chest.

I thought about my father when I told him I was going into the army. We were sitting around the breakfast table, the orange sunlight streaming in through the window. He'd cried too. I guess when sons go off to war, fathers cry. It was true in my kitchen and it was true all the way over here in Belgium. I wondered if there was a time when Yutz's master had a father cry over him. I couldn't picture it, but I guess even Nazis have fathers.

"Time to go, Yutz," I whispered to the dog as I untied his leash from the post. I went to wrap a loop of it over his snout again, but he looked so peaceful lying there, his side rising and falling with each breath, a little snort escaping his snout, I couldn't bring myself to do it again. "You be good this time," I said to him. "Remember the water I gave you."

I jostled the leash to wake him. He sat up instantly, eyes alert, ears perked, tail pointed. His nose worked the air. A soldier dog at attention.

He sniffed at my coat and his little nub of a tail wagged. It must have taken him a second to remember where he was and who he was with, because once he got a sniff of my hand, his ears sagged a little and his behind flopped back onto the floor. He looked me up and down and he sighed. I hadn't known that dogs *could* sigh, but he sure did. Sighing was better than attacking, though, and with another tug on the leash, he stood. It was time to go.

Hugo's father peeked out of the barn. He whistled a short tune, and a moment later, we heard a short tune whistled back from down in the village. He turned back and waved us outside. Hugo went first. When I passed by, Michel patted me on the shoulder.

"Good luck to you and to your countrymen," he said.

"And you and yours," I told him.

Hugo had run out in front and beckoned impatiently for me to follow him.

"With Hugo on our side, we cannot fail." Michel smiled.

Yutz sniffed at Michel as he passed, and Michel slipped a piece of sausage into the dog's mouth. "Maybe this dog will remember Belgium more fondly now." He laughed.

I looked down at the burned and ruined village, the bonfire of old furniture in the square and the patch of Mike's blood in the snow. The villagers must have taken the body to bury it. I couldn't believe this man could still find the strength to laugh in spite of all this ruin.

I saluted him with my free hand, like I would a superior officer, and then I let Yutz pull me to catch up with Hugo. We made our way through the village to the road.

Yutz sniffed at the ground and tried to pull me faster and faster, but I held him back. We had to follow Hugo, not sprint ahead of him.

We didn't stay long on the road. We turned off to the side, through a thick hedge, and scurried like nervous lizards from one overgrown patch of brush to the next.

We crossed a field where no one had plowed and a small village where no one lived. The raised hedges alongside the fields had been crushed and fresh tank treads marred the snow. There were even boot prints frozen in place, like they'd been sculpted in glass. Yutz sniffed at the boot prints and the hair on his back rose. His ears perked and he snarled, sending angry spittle from his floppy lips.

"Not friends of his," I said. "Maybe friends of mine."

Hugo didn't react, either because he didn't understand or because he didn't have the same idea. We moved carefully through the hole in the hedgerow left by the tank.

On the other side, a gruesome scene stretched out before us. From the forest on one side to a hedge on the other, the field was covered in mounds of fresh snow in the length and shape of men. I knew too well what lay beneath. It was like a field of snowmen had been knocked over by a fearsome wind. We moved quickly through the field, watching our steps.

Hugo didn't even look at the lumps, but I could not take my eyes from them. This one had a boot sticking out — American. That one, a German helmet. Yutz sniffed at the mounds, perhaps looking for a familiar smell, and I had to jerk his leash to keep him moving and to keep him from pawing at the snowmen. Though their ends had been violent, at least now they had some peace. I was glad when we left that ghostly battlefield behind. They say that dogs can smell fear. I wonder what Yutz smelled on me.

At dusk, the cloudy sky dimmed and turned a pinkish-gray that made me think of the sergeant in his foxhole. I shuddered. Europe in winter had none of the beauty of my desert sunsets back home in Albuquerque. It just grew dim. Night didn't fall, like they said in books. It spread, like spilled ink. It stained.

We stopped to rest for a moment and Hugo immediately took to petting Yutz. I'd never cared much for dogs, but Hugo, I guess, was fond of them. He looked relaxed as he stroked Yutz's head, pressing back those devilish ears and watching them spring up again. Yutz's nub of a nail wagged so much, his back legs moved.

"How old are you?" I asked Hugo. He looked up at me and smiled.

"Hugo," he said. I guess his English wasn't so good. I had to wonder about him. He was at least a few years younger than me. If we were in the United States, he'd probably be on Christmas break from sixth grade right now. Instead, he was leading me to find the American front lines so I could get help to rescue my friend from the Nazis while his father went off to fight other Nazis. I guess I could no more imagine what his life was like than he could imagine mine. But I had so many questions. Where was his mother? Did he remember what life was like before the war? Did he ever have a dog of his own? Maybe when all this was over, I could give him Yutz. He'd probably want to give the dog a new name, of course. How could I explain any of this to him?

When he saw me staring at him, he smiled and stood from petting the dog.

"We go," he said with a nod, and we were off again, moving quickly through the dark forest.

It didn't take long before we reached a frozen field, and on the other side of it, we could see a road. A river of shadowy men flowed along the road. They moved quickly, coughing and spitting, not speaking, and among them a jeep ground its gears trying to creak along the line. The Germans did not have jeeps like that.

The Americans did.

At first I thought they were marching into battle, taking the fight back to the Germans. Hitler's army had struck the first blow with that early morning sneak attack on our front lines in the forest, but the Americans had regrouped now. I felt a surge of pride to see so many men, rifles on their shoulders, ready to push Hitler out of Belgium and back to Berlin once and for all.

But then I saw the wounded.

Men in stretchers; GIs hobbling, supported by other GIs; men without helmets; men missing coats or boots; men without even their rifles. And then I realized these Americans were in retreat, hundreds of them, rushing as fast as the road could take them away from the battle, away from the Germans.

"Come on," I told Hugo, rising from our position. But the boy placed his hand on my elbow to get my attention. I looked down at him as he saluted me somberly. He'd taken me where I needed to go, and now he had a Resistance to get back to.

I saluted him back, and he nodded before turning around and disappearing into the night as fast as his legs could carry him.

"Okay, Yutz," I told the dog. "Time to meet your enemy."

I let some slack into the leash and Yutz started racing toward the Americans on the road, pulling me behind him, snarling like he was going to take out a whole battalion with just his teeth and claws. In spite of what Michel had said, I was pretty sure he hated Americans.

Too bad for him, because there were a lot of them, and we were about to join up.

I waved my free hand in the air and I called out.

"Hey! Hey! American! USA! USA!"

As I ran across the field, I heard the buzz of a bullet zip past my ear, the snap of rifle shots. I stopped running, pulled Yutz back. He barked and snarled in their direction.

I'd forgotten that I was in a Nazi officer's coat running with a Nazi dog. My own army opened fire on me.

WORLD SERIES WINNERS

"I'm a medic!" I shouted. "American! American!"

I raised one hand in the air. The other held Yutz back as he reared on his back legs, barking and growling. I moved slowly forward, close enough so I didn't have to shout. I kept my head down as a few more shots buzzed by me.

"Don't shoot!" I yelled again. "American!"

When I reached the side of the road, I was staring down the barrels of a half dozen M1 carbine rifles. I had never had a gun pointed at me before in my life. It made me flinch.

"Where you from?" one voice demanded. In the dark, his face was shadow. Yutz barked at him.

"Albuquerque, New Mexico," I told him. "I'm a medic with the Ninety-Ninth."

"Medics don't got no dogs," another voice snapped.

"He ain't dressed like an American," someone added.

"Germans got spies all over," the first voice said. "Shoot him."

"We can't just go shooting him. We're not Krauts. We don't shoot prisoners."

"There's new orders to shoot all SS prisoners on sight."

"He's not a prisoner."

"He might be an American."

"I am!" I pleaded. I tried to open my shirt to show the uniform underneath the civilian clothes, but it was hard to do with one hand, while Yutz was still going nuts. My clothes felt suddenly very thin. The cold wind cut right through them.

"Show your hands!" one of the men yelled.

"Shut that dog up!" another shouted.

"Yutz, quiet!" I yelled, tugging his leash once to get the point across. Much to my surprise, Yutz quieted.

"Who won the 1944 World Series?" one of the men snapped at me.

"What?" I asked. Why was he asking me about the World Series?

"He don't know," one of the others said. "German spy. Shoot him and let's keep moving."

"He just called that dog Yutz."

"That a German word?"

"Sounds like it to me."

"The St. Louis Cardinals!" I answered loudly.

"Who lost?"

"The St. Louis Browns!"

"Not even I knew that," one of the soldiers said.

"Maybe he's a spy who studied the right answers," another said.

"What's a *yutz*?"

"It's . . . uh . . ." I had to remember what Goldsmith called that language. "Yiddish!" I said.

Suddenly, a flashlight flicked on, blinding me.

"Turn that off!" someone farther along the road yelled.

"Light discipline! Full dark!" another yelled.

The light went off.

"We gotta get out of here," a soldier said, shoving the clump of men forward. The river of retreating soldiers flowed around the group that had stopped to talk to me.

"He doesn't look German," a guy said.

"You say you from Albuquerque?"

"Yeah," I answered. I worried how much time I was wasting standing here. Every minute that passed was another minute where Goldsmith and the rest of the prisoners got closer to the trains, closer to the work camp. Closer to the unthinkable.

"You, what, Mexican or something?" I couldn't tell where the voice was coming from. It was too dark and the flashlight had taken out my night vision. I was being interrogated by helmeted shadows.

"I'm American," I said.

"You know what I mean."

"My parents are from Mexico, yeah," I said.

"Speak Spanish."

"What?"

"Prove it."

"Hola," I said, feeling tongue-tied. I didn't know what to say. *"Me llamo Private Miguel Rivera, Ninety-Ninth Infantry. No sé lo que quieres de mí."*

"Was that Spanish?" one of the guys asked.

"Sounded like it to me," another said.

"He could have just made stuff up," said a third.

"Hey, Sanchez!" one of the guys called. "Get Sanchez. We got a guy saying he's Mexican."

"What's up?" A new voice, a new shadow on the line in front of me.

"Guy says he's Mexican, but we don't speak Spanish," they explained.

"He looks Mexican," another said. "Hitler doesn't have any Mexicans in his army, does he?"

"Ask him something in Spanish," they urged the guy named Sanchez.

"¿Quién ganó las World Series en 1944?"

"The St. Louis Cardinals," I told him, frustrated.

"¿Por qué tienes un perro?"

"I took the dog from an SS officer," I said in English. "I'm with the Ninety-Ninth. The Germans overran our position. Took prisoners. I'm trying to help."

The men looked at one another and nodded. They lowered their rifles.

"You can't help 'em if they already got taken," Sanchez said. "We just came from the town of St. Vith. It's a bloodbath, man. They're shooting everyone. Took out an entire battalion. They're even shooting prisoners. It's an SS Panzer Brigade. Tanks and guns and thousands of men. There's no stopping them." He shook his head. "You can't go back that way. We're no match for them. We gotta retreat. Regroup, *hombre*."

"We can't just let them take our guys," I pleaded. "They separated the Jewish soldiers and —" I looked to Sanchez. "And all the ones that looked different. Darker skin. Understand?"

"We got orders to retreat," Sanchez said.

"What's a medic gonna do, anyway?" another guy said. "Take out a Kraut SS division all by himself?"

"Maybe he's no medic. Maybe he's OSS," another suggested.

"You OSS, Rivera?" Sanchez asked. "Some kind of superspy?"

"I'm just a private trying to do the right thing," I said.

Sanchez whistled. "Brave private." The other guys agreed. I felt embarrassed by their admiration. If only they knew how brave I'd been during the first attack, how I'd hidden in a foxhole. They wouldn't think I was so brave then. I looked down at my feet.

"Follow orders, Private," a new voice snapped. "I'm a sergeant and I'm telling you to get on this line and fall back with us."

I ignored the sergeant. I hoped the others might still choose to come with me, though part of me really wanted to go with them. They were older; they were more experienced; they still had officers in charge and orders to follow. They still had each other.

"Should we shoot the dog?" someone asked. I heard the snap of a rifle bolt, saw a gun barrel go up.

"No!" I shouted. I didn't think; I just pulled Yutz behind me, putting myself between danger and the dog. To this day, I couldn't tell you why. Or maybe I could. But I knew right then, I wasn't going to go with these guys. I was going to find my friend.

In the distance, artillery rumbled. Somewhere, the Germans were on the attack, even in the dark of night.

"They'll kill us all," someone else said, shoving past Sanchez.

"Stay or go," said the man who'd called himself a sergeant. "Your funeral."

With a nod, he and the clump of men around him rejoined the flow of retreating soldiers, a river of the wounded and the frightened.

Sanchez stayed still. He looked me over.

"You really gonna take on a squad of SS by yourself?" he asked.

"I'm not by myself," I said. "I've got this dog."

Sanchez shook his head. He slung his rifle off his shoulder and held it out to me. "You're gonna need this," he said.

I took the gun and slung it over my shoulder. "Thanks."

"Good luck," he said, and he vanished back into the river of soldiers.

"To you too," I whispered, watching the shadowy forms of my countrymen slog on down the road. Away from the front lines, away from the German attack, away from the prisoners who needed rescue.

Away from me.

I didn't feel scared watching them go even though I knew they were leaving me all alone. I felt shame instead — a great embarrassment for my country, to be so broken by the Germans, to be humiliated like this, sent into a terrible retreat, like dogs who had tucked their tails between their legs and fled.

I had pulled myself together when I was afraid in my foxhole. I had climbed out, made a plan, taken action. Fear had laid me low, but it didn't beat me. I'd licked it good. Why couldn't these men do the same?

I vowed right then and there that no matter what happened, I would not retreat until I had saved my friend. I would not tuck my tail and run. Never again.

"Come on, Yutz," I told the dog, turning back across the field the way I had come. The dog did not resist. He trotted along at my side, and he didn't even growl. I guess we had a lot in common. Even if we were on opposite sides of this war, we were both soldiers without an army.

OUR TRESPASSES

I had no help. My countrymen were in retreat, Hugo had gone off, probably thinking I'd be safe with the Americans, and my only ally was Yutz, a Nazi war dog.

I was more tired than I think I'd ever been in my life. When was the last time I'd had a real night's sleep? Probably before I joined the army.

The last two days had been the worst of it. My body ached, my left hand felt cramped from holding Yutz's leash for almost thirty-six hours straight, and my cold feet had rubbed themselves raw inside my boots. There was a definite squishing when I walked, and I did not really want to know what was causing it.

I had to take stock of everything I had that could be useful. I had my bag of medic's supplies, the Nazi canteen, the canvas bag with food that Hugo's father had given me, and now, one M1 carbine rifle, fully loaded . . .

I stopped in the field. Yutz stopped at my side, sniffing the ground at his feet. I slid the rifle off my shoulder and balanced it against my hip with my leash hand. Then I used my other hand to check the rifle's ammo magazine. It was like I'd feared. It wasn't fully loaded at all. The magazine was empty.

I pulled back the bolt and checked the chamber. There was one bullet in it.

Great. I had a rifle with one bullet.

If I could figure out how to get him on my side, Yutz would be a more valuable weapon than this rifle.

But that was a big *if.* He tolerated me now, but I wasn't sure it went beyond that. I think the dog knew he was far from home and he needed me. As the snow kept falling, covering our tracks, dusting our clothes with powder, and chilling me to the bone, I knew that I was very, very far from home too. And I needed him.

I slung the rifle back onto my shoulder and made my way across the field to the hedge. In the distance, I heard the thump of artillery, but I couldn't tell if it was American artillery firing at the Germans or German artillery firing at the Americans.

I thought back to the day before, the morning when I found myself on the wrong end of the incoming artillery shells as the earth shook and the trees exploded. The bright orange flashes against the crisp white snow. The bloody footprints my boots left. The screams of terrified men.

I hoped it wasn't our guys on the receiving end this time. I guess that meant I hoped it was German guys getting shelled. The things war makes you wish on other people.

I wondered how I was supposed to find the prisoners now. Hugo had gone too soon. I had no guide. The German and American front lines were moving, and I didn't even know who I might run into next. More Americans? The German Army? How would I ever find the right way?

I kept moving, back in the direction I had come with Hugo. Up ahead, I saw the path of wreckage left by the tank, and I knew what I would find in that field on the other side. The snowmen. I wanted to go around it. I did not want to have to cross that place where German and American boys lay frozen, side by side.

But Yutz whimpered and tugged me in that direction.

He was a willful dog and he knew the scent of war well. I was new to this. He was a veteran, and he knew what to do.

I let Yutz lead me into the field of snowmen, and I let him lead me to the first mound of snow that interested him. He sniffed at it and whined, and I knelt down beside it. He looked up at me and shifted his weight from foot to foot.

"Don't attack me, Yutz," I told him.

I let go of the leash. I needed both hands for what I was about to do.

Yutz didn't move. He sniffed at the mound of snow.

I took out the sharp scissors from my medic's bag and I closed my eyes.

"Padre nuestro, que estás en el cielo." I said the Lord's Prayer like my mother had taught me, or at least I said it as best as I could remember it. I skipped some, but the part I needed came to me. *"Perdona nuestras ofensas, como también nosotros perdonamos a los que nos ofenden."* Forgive us our trespasses, as we forgive those who trespass against us.

With that, I reached my hand into the snow and found the rigid sleeve of a German officer's coat. As I suspected, it was an SS man, just as Yutz's master had been. He was loyal, this dog, even to the dead.

Perdona nuestras ofensas, I thought again. Forgive us.

I tugged the whole arm free of the snow, and, moving as quickly as I could, ignoring Yutz's threatening growl beside me, I cut a square of fabric from the coat.

When it was done, I let the sleeve go and grabbed Yutz's leash again. My fingers stung in the cold, but they wrapped around the leash with ease. Already, it had come to feel like an extension of my arm.

With the other hand I held the cloth up to Yutz's nose. He sniffed it eagerly, and his ears perked; his tail even wagged.

"Okay, pal, you lead the way," I said. "Go get 'em!"

He looked at me funny. I wished I knew how to say *go* or *get* or *'em* in German. All I knew was one phrase, but I guess it was better than nothing. Sometimes, the sound of familiar words is enough to take you home, even if they don't make sense.

"Nicht schiessen!" I said, and Yutz's ears twitched, hearing his familiar language.

He took off, dragging me behind him toward the forest at the far end of the field, away from the sound of artillery fire and deeper into enemy territory.

A BONE TO PICK

The forest was impossibly dark, but Yutz pulled me through the snow with furious speed. I had to trust his instincts, because my own were useless. My instincts told me to hide, back down, retreat. But Yutz led me, sniffing from tree to tree, smelling the ground and the shrubs and the rocks beneath the snow. Dogs do not retreat.

"Be like Yutz," I reminded myself. "Be like Yutz."

I meant, of course, be brave and tough like him, not be a Nazi. Or pee on trees, which he was presently doing.

Every few minutes, he would circle back, smell the cloth I held in my hand, and then run on.

He hadn't thought to growl at me in hours, and I figured things were going well, when he stopped to sniff at a big mound of snow with odd bits of metal sticking out.

He circled around the mound, sniffing and whining. When he pulled me to the other side of the snowy heap, I saw that it was the wreck of a German motorcycle, tilted on its side, with its sidecar partially dug into the ground where it had crashed.

Yutz sniffed at the empty sidecar. Whoever had crashed the motorcycle in the forest was long gone now. I wondered how long it had been wrecked here. I brushed some of the snow away with my sleeve. There were flecks of rust on the spokes of its wheels and some of the paint was chipped, but the blue-and-white logo of the manufacturer was still crisp and clear, as was the Nazi swastika painted on the side.

Yutz gave it another sniff and then spun in a circle at the end of the leash, spinning three times before curling up beside the half-buried sidecar.

"Come on, Yutz," I said. "We don't have time to rest. Don't you want to find your masters again?" I asked, as if he could respond to me or even understand.

He looked at me, snorted, and rested his head on his paws. I tugged the leash, but he stayed put. I knew I couldn't pull him. He was too heavy, too strong, and too determined to go no farther.

"I guess you're the boss," I said, and leaned against the wreck to catch my breath.

Now that we had stopped moving, the cold cut into me again. The wind in the forest wasn't so bad, but the air bit at my lungs every time I inhaled, and it made a frosty cloud in front of me every time I exhaled. My muscles ached, my fingers and toes tingled, and exhaustion swept through me like the German Army had swept through the American front lines.

In my medic's training I'd learned to recognize frostbite (the tingle in my fingers was an early sign) and hypothermia (my drowsiness could be one of the first symptoms). Of course, my drowsiness could also just be from not having slept in days.

Maybe Yutz was right. What good would either of us be if we ran ourselves to death? I needed to sleep, to rest at least for a little bit. But I was worried that if I sat down, I would get hypothermia from the extreme cold and never get up again. I wondered, Would they ever find me in the forest here?

Yutz looked so serene, curled around himself with the overturned motorcycle to shield him from the wind. His dark black fur shined in the night.

The fur, I thought.

I knew what I had to do to keep myself warm.

I had to see how close Yutz would let me get to him. I had to snuggle with the enemy.

I squatted down beside him. His eyes twitched, half open, but he didn't move. I leaned back and sat in the snow, stretching my legs out in front of me.

Still he didn't move.

I leaned in toward him, reaching up to wrap myself around him.

He moved.

In a flash, his head was up, his teeth bared and the black hairs on his back sticking straight up. He growled and snarled and I fell back away from him, losing my grip on the leash. He jumped at me. I blocked him with my raised arm. His teeth wrapped around my sleeve and he bit down. The pain was intense, but with the thick German coat over my uniform, his teeth didn't tear through.

"Off! Bad!" I yelled, but those weren't words to which Yutz responded. His eyes bulged and rolled back in his head in a ferocious mask of rage. His pink gums flared like flames around my arm. He tugged and slashed his head from side to side, wrenching my shoulder. It felt like he would rip my arm off if I didn't stop him.

At least I wasn't cold anymore.

The dog pressed me down on my back with his front paws on my chest. He didn't release my arm, but he stopped thrashing and he didn't bite through. It was more like he was holding me in place. He growled, his lips curling up so I could see the full length of his teeth.

"You win," I said, trying to sound calm. "Good boy. It's okay, I surrender." I cooed and praised. It didn't matter what I said; I just hoped the tone of my voice would relax him, would stop him from biting me. If he went for my throat, that'd be the end of me.

I thought about my rifle lying in the snow beneath me, pressing into my shoulder blade. If I could get it out from under me, there was one bullet in the chamber. Would one bullet be enough to stop this mad dog? Could I bring myself to put a bullet in him?

Suddenly, Yutz let go of my arm and lifted his face to mine. I could smell his breath, felt its warmth on the tip of my nose. His dark eyes shined with intelligence, but not mercy, and I felt at that moment like I was being judged.

I can't explain it, but I felt like the dog saw my whole life — how I hated to hear my parents speak Spanish in public because I was afraid people would think I wasn't really

American; how I signed up for the army against their wishes because I wanted to prove how American I was, and how tough; how I panicked in the foxhole with the dead sergeant, freezing up; how my legs wouldn't move me back into the battle because, to be honest, I did not want them to; how I failed to fight and how even the men I'd tried to bandage and heal were dead; how I was a bad soldier and a bad medic; and how even that little boy Hugo was braver than I was. This dog could see it all. He could see that I was a coward and that my foolish mission to rescue my friend was doomed.

Maybe he didn't see it; maybe he smelled it, because his nostrils twitched once, twice, three times, and then he looked away from me, looked to the forest, where he seemed to find more interesting sights and smells than I could offer.

I had been sized up by this dog and I had been found lacking.

Suddenly, with a quick snap from his jaws, he turned back to me and snatched the piece of cloth from the German's coat from my hand. Then he climbed off of me and trotted away with it in his teeth. I thought he might disappear into the dark, leaving me behind, alone and lost in the woods, but he went back to his burrow beside the wrecked motorcycle, and curled up with the square of fabric, like a child with a blankie.

Our fight was over. I had lost.

My arm was sore where his teeth had gripped me, and I lay where he'd knocked me onto my back, catching my breath and trying to slow my heartbeat. He could have killed me, but he didn't. He could have wounded me badly, but he didn't do that either. And he didn't run away, which he could have easily done. His leash left a slithering line in the snow where he had trailed it, but he hadn't run.

Maybe I'd needed to fight him and I'd needed to lose.

Yutz was a proud dog, trained to obey one master, a master from whom I had taken him, and all my tugging him around had put him to shame. Could dogs feel shame?

I didn't know. I knew humans could. I knew I did.

And that was why he didn't trust me. He could smell my shame. He needed a master, not a coward. If I wanted his loyalty, I had to show him that I was not afraid. I had to show my trust before he would show his.

It was time to put the past behind me and focus on the future. Maybe now that we'd fought, Yutz could put the past behind him too.

"If at first you don't succeed," I grunted, lifting myself from the cold ground and brushing the snow off my chest and my pants. "Try, try again."

Yutz opened his eyes and looked at me. I decided not to come straight at him this time. I didn't want him to think I was challenging him to a rematch.

I approached from the side, my hands open, moving slowly. He lifted his head to watch me, the cloth still dangling from his mouth. He growled and I stopped moving.

"It's okay, Yutz," I said. "You won. You're the boss." I stood still and let him look me over. I didn't feel the same burning shame as he looked at me. I just let him look.

I took another step forward. "It's okay," I repeated.

He didn't growl. He watched me. When I got next to him, I let out a slow breath and prepared myself for another attack. I knelt down beside him. I put my hand out for him to smell it.

He sniffed a few times. His ears twitched, and he looked up at me, his eyebrows raised. His lips didn't tremble and he didn't show his teeth. He exhaled and let his head flop down into the snow. I stretched my hand out and placed it on his side and I stroked his fur. He stretched and rolled, exposing his belly to me. Now that he'd beaten me, he trusted me to rub his belly.

I obeyed, happily.

His fur was soft and warm, passing through my fingers, calming the itch and the ache from the cold. I knelt there in the dark forest petting him, smoothing his fur and rubbing his belly for a long time.

There is some kind of magic in petting a dog, I think. While I petted him, I felt safe for the first time since the German attack. If anyone passed by, I figured the wreck of the motorcycle hid us well enough. As I petted him, I started to feel hopeful. I felt like I could find Goldsmith again, that I could save my friend, and that maybe, when this war was over, the world might just find a way to be all right, in spite of all the death and horror, if everyone could just a pet a dog.

I relaxed.

I don't know for how long I sat there petting him, scratching behind his ears and daydreaming, but the next thing I knew, it was light out and I was lying on the ground with my head on Yutz's side like a pillow, rising and falling with each of his breaths. The sky above the forest was light and the snow glared bright white around me. My body was stiff and I rubbed the sleep from my eyes.

Yutz stretched his limbs and snuffled at my head with his nose, knocking me off of him.

"Okay, okay," I grumbled. "I'm up. . . . You want breakfast?"

I opened my canvas bag and unwrapped one of the sausages. It was frozen solid, so it was easy to snap in half. It didn't look so appetizing to me, but Yutz ate his in one bite. I had to gnaw mine for a while to soften it. I felt like a dog chewing on a bone.

Yutz pawed at the square of cloth on the ground, but he didn't pick it up again, so I bent down and grabbed it, shoving it into my pocket. Then I bent to get his leash and he growled when my hand went for it.

I froze.

"I thought we were past all this?" I said. My arm still ached from last night.

His low rumbling growl sent a shiver up my spine. The leash was just inches from my fingertips.

"Come on, Yutz, we have work to do." I reached for the leash. I didn't think we could lose any more time. We'd already lost hours by sleeping, and for all I knew, the Germans could have already gotten their prisoners to the train depot.

Yutz barked, and from the corner of my eye, I saw him lean back on his haunches, preparing to leap, his ears pointed straight up like devil horns.

"Easy, boy," I said, even as I braced myself for another dog attack.

He barked and sprang into the air, but it wasn't me he was aiming for.

It was the soldier sneaking up behind me.

LOOK TO THE SKY

"*Aiee!*" the man yelled as Yutz sprang through the air and crashed into his chest. The soldier held his hands up to protect himself, just as I had, and Yutz's teeth wrapped around his forearm, yanking him down to the ground, just like he'd done to me.

I swung the rifle off my shoulder and pointed it at the soldier. He had on camouflage but no helmet, and I didn't see any markings on his uniform. He wasn't with the German Army and he wasn't American.

He also wasn't alone.

Another soldier came running through the trees and I raised my rifle, my finger on the trigger, about to put my one and only bullet to use, the first time I had ever pointed a gun at a living thing in my entire life, when Hugo came running through the snow.

"Non! Non!" Hugo yelled.

His father ran behind him, his own rifle in his arms, and four other men shuffled behind them, all dressed for war and all armed for war. These were Resistance fighters.

I lowered my gun. I hoped the fighters hadn't noticed that my hands were shaking.

Yutz looked at the approaching group. I saw his jaw relax around, but not release, the soldier's arm.

"It's okay, Yutz," I told him. "They're friends."

He looked back at me, still growling. All his training told him that he had the enemy in his jaws. All his training told him to attack. But we'd turned a corner, I thought. We had an understanding now.

His body shuddered with the urge to bite.

"It's okay," I repeated at him.

He didn't bite. He released the man's arm and climbed off of him, circling back to me. The man rubbed his wrist. I winced in sympathy. I knew how much Yutz's bite hurt.

Yutz sat beside my heel and looked up at me, like I had looked up at that sergeant when he'd first put me in my foxhole with Goldsmith. The look asked, "Okay, now what?" The look wanted someone to be in charge. I guess Yutz needed a new master and, well, I was it.

"You've learned to trust your dog, no?" Michel said as he shook my hand.

"Maybe he learned to trust me," I said.

"The war dog is like a bullet that you can call back even after it has been fired."

I looked down at Yutz. His long black face, his brown paws, the broad chest, and the ears that pointed up like devil horns. The searching eyes. I couldn't think of him like a weapon, like just one more bullet in my gun. He was as much a soldier as I was. More of one, really.

"How did you find me?" I asked Michel.

"Hugo came back, told us that your American friends would not help you," Michel said. Hugo smiled, knowing that his father was proud of him and was sharing that pride with the American stranger. I nodded my thanks to Hugo. He saluted. "And I thought that no young soldier should be without help on a dangerous mission. But I see that you are not entirely without help."

Yutz scratched behind his ear with his back paw, waiting

for something to happen. He didn't even look at the man he'd knocked down. Dogs didn't dwell on the past. That was a trait reserved just for humans, like worry and regret.

"Yutz is leading me," I said, pulling the cloth square from the Nazi jacket out of my pocket. Yutz's eyes followed it as I held it out to Michel. When his fingers touched it, Yutz growled and I put it away again.

"Very good," said Michel. "We will come with you."

"I want to ask you something." I leaned in to whisper to Michel. "About Hugo . . . Doesn't he have anyone he could stay with?"

Michel nodded. "His grandparents are not so far from here, and when peace comes, we will live with them together. But now, he wishes to fight the Nazis. I could not stop him if I wanted to."

"But this will be dangerous," I said.

"To live in these times is dangerous," Michel answered. "To live only for yourself is dangerous. Hugo understands this. As I believe you understand this too."

He patted me on the shoulder. I fought the urge to hug him. He made me think again of my own father, of how much I hoped to return to him, but also, how I hoped he would be proud of what I was doing now. I could have run away, but instead I was running into danger. I was running to help my friend. And these men and this one brave boy were here to help.

My heart pounded in my chest. I had been in the war for only a few days, and now I was leading a group of Resistance fighters to attack a Nazi prisoner convoy. I hoped that I was up to the job and that Yutz wouldn't let me down . . . or betray me.

There was only one way to find out, and every second that passed was another second that Goldsmith and the rest of the prisoners were farther away.

"Let's go," I said. I stooped to grab Yutz's leash and our eyes met. He didn't growl at me, but I stopped.

Trust.

He trusted me now. I guessed I had to trust him.

I unclipped the leash from his collar.

I let him sniff the cloth square again. His stubby tail started wagging. He took in a few deep snorts of the cloth, then sniffed at the ground and at the air and barked with excitement.

He shot off, running ahead with his front and back legs pumping in unison, moving faster than any of us could hope to run. He vanished into the forest ahead and I feared I'd lost him. I'd trusted too much and forgotten that he was a German dog, that he belonged to the SS, and that like all dogs, his greatest desire was to run home.

But from the forest ahead, I heard a bark. I ran toward it, the Resistance fighters running with me, and there was Yutz, standing with one paw raised, waiting for us. The moment he saw us, he barked again and ran on, leading us forward, pausing every few minutes. I realized that his paw prints in the snow made it easier to follow him, and we didn't have to stop to listen for him so often. He could run and we could follow, and like that, we would find our way to the prisoners.

The physical activity burned our lungs, but it kept us from freezing, and by afternoon, the snow had stopped and the sky had started to clear. As we left the forest for the open countryside, Yutz stopped to rest. We all gathered around and enjoyed the feeling of sun on our faces. We ate bread and caught our breath. The man Yutz had attacked rubbed his wrist and kept his distance from the dog. The others talked to one another in low voices and scanned the surrounding fields for signs of danger.

I looked at Yutz, who was panting, his ears perked. He looked at the sky, fully alert. A moment later, we heard what he had heard already. The high-pitched whine of an airplane overhead. First one, then another, then more.

I searched the sky and saw the shimmering of sunlight off of metal as a squadron of American fighter planes zoomed over the countryside. We could see them over the forest, and we watched them dive, firing off their heavy guns at some unseen German position below.

The Resistance fighters cheered at the sound of the guns. Hugo grinned and pointed, made airplane noises. He jumped up and down with excitement. I couldn't help but smile too.

"The weather has turned against the Nazis," Michel smiled. "With American planes in the sky, Hitler's attack cannot succeed."

We stood a moment, taking in the sight of the planes overhead, the trails of their exhaust drawing squiggles and zigzags of white cloud against the sky. The whine of their engines, circling and swinging down over the forest, was like music to our ears.

Miles away, we saw large cargo planes dropping supplies with parachutes onto American positions. We saw high-flying bombers pounding what must have been German tank squadrons or artillery positions, perhaps the same ones that had first led the attack. Hitler was no match for the might of the US Air Force.

Watching the planes rain down deadly fire, I couldn't help but imagine the German soldiers curled in their fox-holes or cowering beside their burning tanks. A merciless thought crossed my mind, true enough, but terrible all the same: Better them than me.

The planes were far away, supporting the Americans on the front lines. It was the first time I could see how far I had come into German controlled territory. The Germans had pushed the American army back several miles while Yutz and I had run miles in the opposite direction.

I realized that once we found Goldsmith, even if we could liberate him from the SS, we would still have to get back to friendly territory somehow without running into the German Army or being recaptured.

"Ruff! Ruff!" Yutz hopped to his feet, barking, ready to go. He started off, but only made it a few yards when he turned around and looked to me. "Ruff!" he barked again. Worried as I was, I had to smile. He wasn't going to leave without me.

We ran, cutting through the forest, maybe another mile, maybe ten. It was hard to tell. My legs ached. Running through the snow was harder than running on normal ground. My feet were soaked when we reached the edge of the forest. Yutz had stopped to mark another tree when Michel came up beside me.

"You should put this dog back on his leash," he said.

I didn't know why at first, but he pointed down a hill to the stretch of train tracks beyond it, and not far away, the train depot. One low building with a guard tower and a ring of barbed wire around it.

A train sat in the station, rumbling, and beside it stood a couple of German soldiers, stomping their feet to keep warm. Just beyond them, I saw the Americans, looking pale and weary. Their faces were muddy, their clothes in tatters, and their feet bare. I couldn't see all of them, but I searched the row of faces for Goldsmith.

I couldn't find him.

But I did see the SS dog handler with his big German shepherd dog.

I grabbed Yutz and clipped his leash onto his leather collar as quickly as I could. He looked up at me and lowered his ears flat against his head — a look of disappointment, it seemed to me. I pulled him back to the cover of the trees, before the Germans could see us. We needed time to make a plan, to figure out how we would free the prisoners. They were under heavy guard.

From where I crouched with Yutz, I could hear a train door open, and I watched as they loaded the Americans inside, one by one. As they went, the healthy soldiers helped the wounded ones up, passing them to the men who were already inside the train car.

That's when I saw Goldsmith limp forward. He'd been injured somehow. He grimaced with pain as he was lifted onto the train. His left foot was swollen and black. He needed a medic, but I doubted the Nazis would give him one.

I had to get to him before it was too late.

I saw Obersturmführer Schultz shouting orders and two other SS men slammed the train door shut and locked it. I could hear the Americans inside yelling and groaning, packed too tightly in the dark train car that had originally been built for transporting cattle, not men. The men of the SS shouted at them and then climbed aboard a different train car, one that had been made for passengers. The dog handler did a walk around the whole train while his dog sniffed at everything, and then he too climbed aboard.

Even Yutz knew they were about to get away. He strained at his leash and whimpered.

I turned to Michel, who crouched beside me with little Hugo at his shoulder, both of them eyeing the train depot.

"They will not move the train while the American planes are in the sky," Michel explained. "We still have some time."

Then Hugo looked at me, his cheeks and nose bright red from the cold.

"We will stop the train?" he asked.

I nodded. "We will stop the train."

I even had an idea of how we could do it, but we'd need to move quickly.

"First," I said, "do any of you know how to fix a broken motorcycle?"

LIKE RIDING A BIKE

All but four German soldiers were aboard the train. One remained up in the guard tower, watching over the tracks and the train depot with a large machine gun. The other three stood around with their rifles on their shoulders, waiting for the train to pull out and for peace to return to the quiet country train station.

The four guards were not the fearsome men of the SS. They were regular German Army soldiers, the kinds of guys I might have been if I'd been born in Germany instead of New Mexico. I gazed through a pair of binoculars I'd borrowed from Michel.

As I looked closer at the soldiers standing on the platform, I saw that they actually weren't much like me at all.

They weren't much like any soldiers in the United States Army. Two of them were old men, gray haired and stoop shouldered. The other one was a boy about Hugo's age. His pants were too big, and his coat hung off him almost to the ground. I couldn't tell about the guy in the tower, but I could guess. All the healthy young men my age were off at the front lines fighting the war. Lucky for us, guarding train stations wasn't very important to Hitler, so he didn't put his best troops on the job. These German soldiers looked anxious, waiting for the train to leave. I wondered if the SS frightened them as much as they frightened me.

In the distance, I heard the whine of the airplane engines, but I couldn't see them in the sky anymore. The German soldiers looked up too. The engine sounds faded. The bombing runs were over, and the planes were on their way back to England to refuel and reload. The train engine hissed and chugged and, with a loud screech, the train pulled inch by inch out of the station.

I held my breath. Yutz panted beside me. Even though it was freezing out, his tongue hung long and pink from the side of his mouth. He shifted on his paws and moved like he wanted to chase the train.

"You'll get your chance," I told him.

I waited for the train to speed up. It pulled from the station and I watched it go, pistons chugging, steam rising. For my plan to work, the train had to be far enough away from the depot to be out of the machine gunner's sight.

From where I was hidden among the trees, I couldn't see Michel or Hugo or the other Resistance fighters. I had to hope they could get in position farther down the track fast enough. Once my plan started, there would be no going back. If they weren't there in time, I was doomed, along with Goldsmith and the other prisoners.

I ran my arm down the gray front of the German officer's coat, feeling for the first time like my outfit was a disguise. Then I gripped the handlebars of the motorcycle tight in my fists, and I kicked the engine to life.

When it revved and roared, I let out my breath. At least it worked. In the sidecar of the motorcycle, Yutz barked, and I shifted into gear.

We shot from the forest with a roar and zoomed down a small slope. I glanced at the German soldiers as I raced alongside the tracks and past the train station and gave them the famous Nazi salute, one arm raised high with my palm flat out in front. Driving one-handed, the bike wobbled and

I almost lost control, but they must not have noticed, because they returned my salute as I zoomed by. As far as they knew, I was a German officer with a dog racing to catch up to the train I'd just missed.

So far, so good.

Now we just had to catch the train.

I squeezed the throttle and sped the motorcycle, bouncing Yutz up and down on the icy terrain by the side of the railroad track. Since the snow had stopped falling and the air was still freezing cold, I was driving on packed and slippery ice. I could feel the wheels skidding and sliding beneath me, and I did my best to keep from crashing into the tracks or flipping over sideways. I didn't dare look back to see if the German soldiers had noticed that I drove like someone who had never been on a motorcycle before. In truth, I hadn't.

I drove as fast as I could. Yutz lifted his nose to the air and held his mouth slightly open so that his tongue flapped in the breeze like a banner. I didn't know if dogs could smile, but it sure looked like Yutz had a grin on his face. He seemed comfortable in the sidecar and with the wind in his face, and I realized then that even though it was my first time on a motorcycle, it might not have been Yutz's. I almost wished he could do the driving.

We followed a bend in the tracks that cut through more forest, taking us out of sight of the train station and the watchtower. Up ahead, I saw the back of the train chugging along. I lowered my head so the wind wouldn't blow so strongly into my eyes and so any SS soldiers guarding the back of the train wouldn't be able to get a good look at me. I was too short and too dark-skinned to be a Nazi. As long as I moved fast, I hoped I could slip past them and buy enough time to spring our trap.

I steered a little bit wide of the tracks. Trees whipped by beside me, and I had to duck to avoid getting my head taken off by the branches. I jerked the bike away from the woods and heard the sickening scrape of metal on metal. Sparks flew.

Yutz flinched to the side and then gave me a snarling look. I'd gotten too close to the tracks on his side.

"You want to drive?" I snapped at the dog, and leaned forward, squeezing the throttle harder. It pinched my fingers, but I was gaining on the train. I saw the face of one of the SS soldiers appear at the railing of the caboose, all the way at the back. He wore his long gray coat open, and it flapped in the breeze. He held a submachine gun in his hands, and he watched me approach, his finger on the trigger.

I gave the Nazi salute again, keeping my head down and doing my best to keep the motorcycle steady. He returned the salute, and I accelerated. I could feel the officer's eyes watching as I drove by the caboose.

I had to get to the front of the train quickly now, before he wondered why I didn't have a helmet or goggles like a motorcycle driver normally would.

"Here we go," I told Yutz. He couldn't hear me over the breeze, but he looked ready. His tongue no longer flapped from his mouth. His eyes were fixed straight ahead, ears pointed and alert. He'd been bred for battle, and I suppose he could sense that it was coming.

I still didn't know whose side he would be on.

DOG TRAINING

I glanced at the cattle cars as I sped past them.

I passed several freight cars and a flatbed car with a large antiaircraft gun on it and a few cattle cars, one of them holding the American soldiers on their way to a death camp.

As I approached the engine at the front, I saw another SS man step out to the metal railing on its side. He did not look happy to step out into the cold wind.

His machine gun rested on his shoulder and his head cocked to the side. It reminded me of Yutz looking puzzled. I waved my arm, trying to signal him to slow the train. He shouted something, but I couldn't hear it over the roar of the train and the rumble of the motorcycle.

He shouted again and waved me closer. I sped up and eased myself as close as I dared to the side of the engine. Yutz kept his eyes up, on the officer. I knew the guy was only letting me get so near to the train because he thought I was on his side. If he got a good look at me or asked me a question, my whole disguise would fall apart. But still, he waved me closer.

My motorcycle bounced along next to the train, so close that the SS man could easily have bent down to pet Yutz in the sidecar.

"Was ist los?" he yelled. I kept my eyes focused forward. I had to keep the motorcycle from crashing. I didn't answer. I tried to make some sort of signal to get him to stop the train. He must not have understood, because he shouted again, but I had to weave away from the train to dodge a tree branch, and I didn't hear him.

I guess he got the view he needed of me, because when I came back in close once more, waving my arm at him, he raised his machine gun at me. I saw his mouth move in a shout, but the words were sucked away by the wind.

The train track was slightly higher than the ground next to it, and my wheels were slipping down the icy slope. I was below the train, with the SS officer looking down on Yutz and me. He shouted again, and this time, he fired his gun. I heard a bullet whizz over my head.

My plan wasn't going at all like I'd planned it.

But if the train got away, Goldsmith and all those prisoners would be lost. I had to stop this train. I had to stop it now.

I steered the motorcycle alongside the train, going slower and then faster and then slower again so that the SS man couldn't aim at me easily. I knew I would have only one chance at this. Using all the power I could get from the motorcycle's engine and leaning hard toward the side, I skittered up the slope until we were right next to the train, right below the barrel of the Nazi's gun.

"Nicht schiessen!" I yelled up at him. The SS man hesitated. He understood "don't shoot."

But so did Yutz. And he knew it meant I was in danger.

With a bark, Yutz took a flying leap from the sidecar of the motorcycle, up over the railing of the train.

The SS man screamed as Yutz landed on top of him, snarling and snapping and pressing the man flat on his back while his gun clattered away. Sparks flew from the train tracks beside me as the train driver pulled the brakes.

Although I couldn't hear the SS man above the screeching brakes, I could see him struggling and writhing to escape Yutz's grasp.

I knew darn well that he couldn't.

I had to pull away as the train slowed, my motorcycle sliding down the small slope, but I stayed parallel to the train.

It took a long time for the train to come to a full stop, and once it did, I could hear shouts from a cattle car in the center, and the yelling and grunting of the officer struggling beneath Yutz. I heard the dog's growls and snarls, and for the first time, they made me smile.

Yutz was on my side after all.

I climbed off the motorcycle and pulled my rifle with its one bullet from the sidecar. Then I ran up to the engine car and hauled myself over the railing. Yutz didn't even look up at me, he was so focused on his attack. I realized then that I had no idea how to call him off. He would do what he wanted.

I looked to the forest behind the train and I didn't see Michel, little Hugo, or any of the other Resistance fighters. They had left before the train started moving and Hugo had led them to a shortcut, but still, we had gone farther than I'd planned and it would take them some time to catch up. I didn't know how long it would be before the other SS soldiers came forward to find out what was going on and discovered Yutz and me. We couldn't fight a whole squad of armed Nazis on our own, and when the one with the big German shepherd dog showed up, I wasn't even sure if Yutz would stay on my side. Dogs were pack animals, after all, and the SS dog handler would know all the right commands for a Nazi war dog. All I knew how to say was "don't shoot."

"Ach! Hau Ab!" the SS man on his back yelled, struggling to get Yutz to release him. *"Hilfe!"* he yelled. *"Hilf mir!"*

I didn't need to speak German to know he was screaming for help. He wanted me to call the dog off. He wanted to be released. I almost felt bad for the guy, until I remembered that he had just shot at me and that he was taking my friend to a death camp just because he was Jewish.

I turned away from him and tried to open to the door to the engine so that I could demand that the driver tell me which car held the Americans, but the driver had locked the door.

I pounded on it, but he didn't open it. Listening to the SS officer's screams, I couldn't blame him. I wouldn't open the door either.

I jumped down from the engine and ran along the stopped train, shouting.

"Americans! Where are the Americans?" I pounded on the outside of the cattle cars. I ran and I yelled.

"Here!" someone shouted in English from the fourth car. "We're in here!"

"Hold on, guys," I yelled back, feeling heroic, like John Wayne in *Flying Tigers*. I wanted to say something heroic. "Private Miguel Rivera of the Ninety-Ninth Infantry is here to get you out of there!"

A cheer went up inside the cattle car and I smiled. My smile vanished as soon as I heard the shrill voice behind me shout *"Hände hoch!"* which I guess was one more bit of German that I knew. I'd heard it enough lately. It meant: "Hands up."

I glanced over my shoulder and saw the whole group of SS men, including Obersturmführer Schultz, had disembarked from the passenger car near the caboose. There were five of them in all, pointing their guns at me.

Five more that I hadn't seen at all during my recon appeared from a car near the front of the train, pointing their guns at me as well.

"Hilfe! Hilfe!" shouted the SS man by the engine, still at the mercy of the big Doberman pinscher I'd set on him.

One of the soldiers nearby approached with his gun raised, taking aim at Yutz.

"Nein! Halt!" The SS dog handler shouted at him. He and his German shepherd moved in their direction to take control of Yutz and stop his attack.

"Hände hoch!" Schultz commanded me again. He held his Luger pistol steady. It was the same pistol he'd used to shoot Mike in the town square. I had no choice. I had to surrender. As my hands went up, my heart sank.

I'd come so close, overcome so many fears, only to fail. I wondered if they'd just shoot me out here and drive on, or if they'd load me into the cattle car with the rest of the Americans and send me off to the death camps as another prisoner. I wondered what would happen to Yutz, assuming he ever let go of that SS soldier. Would the Nazis shoot him as a traitor? Would they take him back into their ranks? Would he miss me when I was gone?

"Hilfe!" the SS man underneath Yutz shouted.

The other soldier raised his gun at Yutz again.

"Nein! Verstehst du nicht?" The dog handler yelled. *"Nicht schiessen!"*

That was his mistake.

I guess I'd taught my dog a new trick, because in a flash, he'd jumped off his victim and down from the engine, charging away into the woods. The soldier fired after him, but he missed. The German shepherd barked after Yutz, but his master held him back. They did not chase the dog down.

I felt some relief. At least one prisoner escaped today, even if he was my prisoner. He'd earned his freedom, after all.

"American?" Schultz asked me, with hardly a trace of a German accent.

"Private Miguel Rivera, United States Army, Serial Number 38 694 022," I said.

According to our training, if we were captured we were just supposed to say our name, rank, and serial number, nothing else. I slammed my mouth shut and I waited. I wondered if I would hear the bullet before it killed me. I felt my lip quivering. It was embarrassing, but I couldn't help it. I was about to die and I was afraid.

"You are all alone?" The SS officer laughed. "You think you can stop this train all by yourself?"

"Private Miguel Rivera, United States Army, Serial Number 38 694 022," I repeated, but my voice caught in my throat. I was about to cry. I could feel it coming.

"You have dressed in a German Army uniform," Schultz said calmly. "Under the laws of war, I am permitted to shoot you right now."

"Since when do Nazis care about the laws of war?" I snapped at him. It felt good to be defiant. It kept me from crying.

He poked a finger and opened my jacket, looking at my uniform.

"You fight with the Ninety-Ninth Infantry Division," he said, seeing the checkerboard insignia on my sleeve. "I believe your own people call you the Battle Babies."

I said nothing.

"I have killed many of your division," he told me. "Many more will die before you ever reach the Fatherland. You mongrel races are too weak to fight us. That is why you dress up in disguises. That is why your dog ran off. That is why you cry. Perhaps, if you had brought a real soldier with you, you might have lived. But now . . ." He shrugged and then he raised his pistol level with my head. I closed my eyes.

And then, I heard Yutz barking.

JABO!

I opened my eyes and saw that big Nazi war dog of mine leading the Resistance fighters right to us.

When the SS men turned to look, I dropped to the ground and threw myself under the motionless train. The SS officer fired a shot into the dirt as I scrabbled over the tracks and to the other side.

I heard the crack of gunfire as the Resistance and the SS broke out into a firefight.

I hoisted myself out from underneath the train car on the opposite side.

"You've got to come out on this side!" I shouted up to the Americans in the cattle car. "Can you break through the car?"

I saw the wood bulging and heard the crunch of men kicking it, throwing their whole bodies into the wood, but it wouldn't budge. It was built to hold cattle. A few wounded Americans wouldn't be able to break the walls down.

"Ruff! Ruff!" I heard at my feet, and I looked down to see Yutz crawl from beneath the train, panting at my heel.

"Good boy!" I said, patting his head. He let me.

A bullet buzzed over me and I dove to the ground again, pulling Yutz beneath the train once more. I saw the boots of the Nazi SS men moving backward and the boots of the Resistance fighters moving forward. We had them on the run.

We.

I swallowed hard. Here I was again, in battle, and all I could do was hide underneath a train, like a yellow-bellied chicken. A coward. But I was done with that. No more weakness. I'd be as brave as my dog.

My dog.

That's what he was now.

My rifle lay in the dirt beside the train, almost close enough for me to reach. It only had one bullet, but I knew I could use the one bullet for some good. I had to.

I rolled out, throwing myself on top of the rifle and jumping to my feet. Like a good soldier, Yutz was right there beside me. Bullets hit the wood above my head, sending hot splinters through the air. I felt the sting of one slicing my ear.

That was just like me, to get wounded by a splinter during a gunfight.

I crouched down below the big latch on the cattle-car door and I aimed my rifle up.

"Stand back!" I yelled, and fired my one and only bullet. My first shot of the war.

The latch blasted off, and I heaved the door open. Inside, men in US Army uniforms huddled together.

A rattle of machine-gun fire sent them diving away from the door and sent me hurling myself back to the ground.

"You must find cover!" Michel yelled at me from between two train cars. He fired a few blasts from his rifle toward the Nazis by the front of the train, who returned fire just as eagerly. I was stuck in the middle with the American prisoners. If they got off the train now, they'd be cut down in the crossfire.

Michel signaled another of his fighters, who was off to the side of the tracks, firing from behind a tree. The man opened fire at the Nazis to give us some time to get to the woods.

"Go, now," Michel said. "You must —"

Suddenly, he fell forward to his knees from his spot between the train cars. A dot of blood grew on his chest. His mouth opened slightly and a puff of thin, gray smoke came out. He fell on his face into the snow by the tracks, dead.

SS Obersturmführer Schultz stepped from between the cars. He'd snuck around the far side. The fighter by the tree had been flanked as well. Two regular German Army guys had him at gunpoint with his hands in the air. I recognized them — they were the kids from the train depot. With a nod from the SS officer, the boys shot the Resistance fighter.

I looked around frantically and I saw the bodies of the other men who had been with Michel, all of them lying in the snow, dead. All of them but Hugo. I couldn't see the boy. I hoped he had gone. I hoped he had not seen his father killed in battle.

The other SS soldiers moved back down the train and pointed their machine guns into the open train car, where the American prisoners put their hands up. They were helpless inside there. A single machine gunner could mow them all down.

The SS officer thrust his gun into my face.

"Where did you steal this dog?" he demanded.

"I didn't steal him," I said as calmly as I could. "He came with me. He wants to be on the winning side."

The SS officer said something in German to others, who grumbled and chuckled derisively.

The dog handler called out a command in German, and Yutz lowered his head, pressed his ears flat back.

"Hier!" the SS man yelled. *"Komm."* He snapped his fingers.

Yutz looked up at me. I could have sworn it looked like he wanted to apologize, but dogs aren't like that. Instead, he trudged away, over to the SS dog handler and his big German shepherd. Yutz was a soldier and he'd been given a direct order. He had to obey.

"It's okay, Yutz," I told him. "It's okay."

My dog sat beside the German shepherd, and somehow, he looked tiny.

"Where in America do you come from?" Obersturmführer Schultz asked me.

"New Mexico," I said. It couldn't hurt to tell him. I was going to die anyway.

"You are Mexican?" he sneered.

"He's American!" a voice above me said. I looked over my shoulder to the cattle car, and saw Goldsmith limp out to the front of the group of prisoners. He didn't have his hands raised. His fists were clenched into angry balls, like he was going to punch his way to freedom. He looked down at me and smiled sadly. "You named your dog Yutz?"

I shrugged. "You should have seen how he was acting, afraid to get out of his foxhole."

"Afraid or smart?" Goldsmith chuckled. We both knew who we were really talking about.

"Touching," said the SS officer. "The Mexican and the Jew will die together."

"We are prisoners of war!" Goldsmith yelled. "Under the laws of war, you cannot simply shoot us and —"

A sound cut him off, a high-pitched whine, like a giant dog calling for his master. The whine grew louder and higher pitched. It came from above and more whines joined it.

The Germans looked up toward the sunset, shielding their eyes. Even Goldsmith looked up, though all he could see was the roof of the cattle car.

"Achtung! Jabo!" one of the SS men shouted and pointed at the sky.

I didn't know what a *jabo* was supposed to be, but the German pointed at a squadron of American Mustang fighter planes coming our way at full speed, guns blazing.

They were over us in seconds.

A few of the SS soldiers scrambled toward the big antiaircraft guns in the center of the train, but they didn't make it in time. The first line of bullets sliced right through them. The hail of fire that followed sent the cluster of German soldiers in front of me, sprawling and scattering in every direction. For a moment, I thought we'd been saved.

A bomb struck the caboose and sent dirt, snow, and flames flying into the air, knocking the back of the train sideways off the tracks. The planes swept by overhead and made a wide arc in the sky, coming straight back at us for another attack run, opening up with their big machine guns and slicing the wood of the train cars to pieces. The GIs hit the deck as the top of their cattle car was turned to Swiss cheese.

That was when I realized that the pilots didn't know that there were Americans down here. They just thought they were shooting up a German military train. We were under attack from our own countrymen and they weren't going to stop until the whole train was destroyed.

"Run!" I yelled. "To the woods!"

The Americans started climbing down out of the train car. The SS men were already running away to take cover. A few of them fired their guns back in our direction, but they didn't take the time to aim, so the shots didn't get anywhere near us.

I grabbed Goldsmith to help him down as the other prisoners were jumping from the train and scattering, just like the Germans. Everyone ran for the woods.

With bullets and bombs all around us, I put Goldsmith's arm around my shoulder and carried him as we scurried for the safety of the forest.

I glanced back at the burning train. SS Obersturmführer Schultz was flat on his back on the ground. At least the upper half of him was. It was anyone's guess where his legs had gone. He'd been blown to bits.

Then I saw the dog handler and his German shepherd. He was running after a small group of Americans. His dog raced ahead and knocked one of them down. The handler ran forward and, without hesitating, shot the American on the ground in the back of the head. Rage boiled inside me. I wanted to chase that Nazi thug down. I wanted him to pay for his cruelty.

But the planes were coming around again and I had to get into the woods and find cover with Goldsmith. They started firing again, their bullets kicking up the snow in long lines, like a giant flaying the earth with a whip. Before I lost sight of the Nazi and his dog, I realized that Yutz was nowhere to be seen.

I hoped that he had run for safety. What if he was wounded? But I had to stay with Goldsmith. He couldn't walk on his own. I saw how black and bruised his bare feet had become. Severe frostbite.

"Come on," I said as we staggered into the forest together.

I'd done what I said I would, anyway. I got Yutz back to his masters. What happened now was up to him. He was a big, mean Nazi war dog, after all.

Still, I wished I'd had the chance to say good-bye.

CHAPTER 18

BOOTS

We rested by a thick growth of fir trees. I set Goldsmith down and caught my breath, glancing back at the black smoke rising from the wreckage of the train and listening to the engine sounds of the American fighter planes fade away as they flew off. Every few seconds, there was a new blast and a pop, like fireworks on the Fourth of July. It was the antiaircraft shells on the train exploding unused in their crates.

The American pilots would go to bed tonight with no idea that they'd nearly killed a whole lot of American GIs. I guess they'd also saved our lives at the same time. Savior and killer were about a razor's width apart when it came to war.

I became pretty sure then and there that I'd just as soon be done with war forever. I decided that if I got Goldsmith and myself back to safety and made it through the rest of this war alive, I'd do my best to spend my life back home in peace, out in the desert in a comfy little place where the snow never stuck and I'd never try to prove anything to anybody again.

"You sprung me, *vato*," Goldsmith said.

"You remembered your Spanish, you *yutz*," I said right back.

He laughed even as it hurt him to laugh. I could see the pain he was in, and I still had my medic's bag with me underneath my German coat. Goldsmith shivered, so I took the coat off and wrapped it around his shoulders.

"Take that off me," he said.

"You're freezing," I said.

"I'd rather freeze than wear a Nazi coat."

Goldsmith was idealistic. I thought he was being pretty foolish. Better to use the coat of the guys that wanted to kill you than to die of frostbite just to spite them. I left it on him and he was too tired to shrug it off. Next I pulled out an ampoule of morphine and shot it into Goldsmith's leg.

"For the pain," I told him.

He nodded and rested his head against the tree, his eyes going a little glassy as the medicine kicked in.

"So, what was with you and that dog?" he asked me.

I told him about how I woke up in the foxhole and everyone was either dead or gone; how I found the dog and figured he could help me; how we hadn't trusted each other at first, but had come to get along; and how he'd really been the one to stop the train.

"You used a Nazi dog to save me," said Goldsmith, laughing. His laugh came out wheezy and started him coughing. When he recovered, he nodded. "That takes some chutzpah."

"Chutzpah?"

He smiled. "You've got guts, is what I'm telling you, *vato*."

"Not me." I rubbed my hands together to warm them. "I just followed the dog."

We heard the popping of machine-gun fire and shouts in German and in English coming through the woods.

"We've got to keep going," I told Goldsmith. "We're a long ways behind German lines. They can still recapture us."

He nodded and I helped him up. The ground was wet and uneven, and it was hard for me to walk carrying most of his weight. Every time he put his bare feet down on the snowy ground, he grunted and winced. We only made it about ten steps before he collapsed and we both tumbled down.

"This isn't going to work," he said. "I won't make it. You have to leave me."

"*Now* you're being a *yutz*," I said. "I'm not leaving you. I'll go back to get some boots."

"Where are you going to find —" he started, but then it dawned on him. Dead men need no boots. I was going back to the train to take a pair. Goldsmith sighed. "Some war, huh?"

"Some war," I agreed. "Stay here."

I ran back to the train tracks, keeping as low as I could, weaving between the trees. Machine guns crackled in the distance. They made me think of chattering teeth. When I reached the edge of the woods, I stopped and ducked behind a tree. I peeked out to make sure it was safe. The train engine billowed black smoke into the sky. The whole back half was burning with bright orange flames, and several of the cars lay on their sides in the white snow.

It was a total wreck. There was no way new trains could pass by until the track was cleared. The Germans wouldn't be able to move supplies and weapons around this way for a while, but that also meant that any new prisoners the

Germans took would have to go on foot. Of course, after this escape, they might decide that taking prisoners was more trouble than it was worth. The thought made me shudder.

I looked over the rows of bodies lying in the snow. It was a strange feeling, trying to decide whose boots I should steal. I felt like a grave robber.

I saw one of the SS officers facedown in the snow. His boots were tall and thick. They looked like they were lined with some kind of fur. I was amazed at how much better the German Army's equipment was. Unlike us, they'd been ready for winter.

I raced out, half-crouched, and I threw myself down to my knees beside the dead Nazi. I began to untie his boots. I yanked the first one off and moved on to the second without pausing to think about what I was doing. Just a few short days ago, the thought of being so close to the dead, of touching them and tearing off their shoes, would have been unimaginable to me. Now, the unimaginable seemed ordinary. I'd love to say that I felt bad about what I was doing, but I didn't feel bad. I didn't feel anything. I just did what I had to do to save my friend.

Once I had the second boot off, I tied them both together by the laces so I could carry them over my shoulder, and

I stood to make my way back to Goldsmith as fast as possible.

That's when I heard the growl behind me.

I froze.

"Yutz?" I said without turning around.

"Grrrrrr." The low rumble again.

I dared a glance over my shoulder.

It wasn't Yutz.

The large German shepherd stood less than five feet from me. I hadn't even heard him approach. His whole body was rigid; the hair on his back stood up, and he lowered his head for an attack.

"Easy . . . easy," I said, remembering too well when Yutz had almost torn me apart. And that was just to teach me a lesson. I didn't think this dog had any lessons in mind. I was the enemy, and he was still a soldier. He wanted me dead.

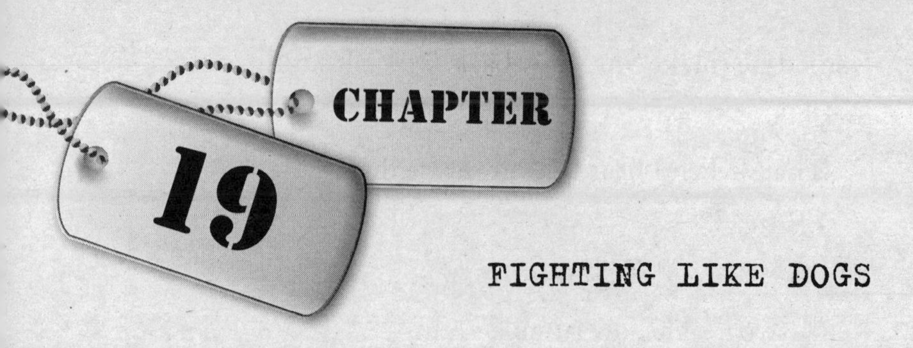

FIGHTING LIKE DOGS

The dog sprang at me. I tried to dive out of the way, but there was no escaping him, and the full weight of the animal crashed into my back, slamming me to the ground. He had knocked the wind out of me, and I gasped for air and squeezed my eyes shut. I waited for the horrible feeling of sharp teeth tearing into me.

Suddenly, there was a snarl and a loud yelp as someone tackled the big dog. I heard a commotion just to my side, and when I opened my eyes, I saw a riot of teeth and fur, spittle flying and the vicious sounds of a dogfight. Yutz and the German shepherd were locked in bloody battle just a foot from where I lay.

Helplessly, I watched them roll.

First Yutz had the other dog pinned and reared his head back to bite the German shepherd's neck. His lips pulled back and his fangs flashed in the sun, but the other dog bucked beneath him and escaped. He snapped at Yutz and swiped at him with his claws. Their faces met; their teeth tore each other's cheeks. The snarls and the barks were wild, like wolves.

Each of them was deep black with brown snouts and paws, and though their bodies were shaped differently, in the tangle of fur and fury, I had trouble telling which dog was which. The black of the fur shined wet and when one dog would roll or fall, he'd leave a bright red streak in the white snow. My heart ached to help Yutz.

I stepped forward, but the dogs rolled and snapped and I couldn't get close enough to interfere.

Suddenly, I saw Yutz twist and clamp his jaws down on the other dog's leg. A terrible yelp went up, so loud and sharp it made the hair on the back of my neck stand up.

The German shepherd fell. He tried to stand, but he couldn't support his own weight. Yutz had broken the dog's leg. They were both dripping blood from their mouths and panting hot breath into the cold air, but Yutz could still stand.

He circled and the big dog snarled at him, turning, trying to keep his face toward Yutz, but his wounds slowed him down. Yutz's ears, though torn and bleeding, still pointed up like devil horns. He was ready to strike. He growled.

The other dog looked away from him. He whimpered and then he lay down and rolled onto his side, exposing his belly to Yutz. He'd surrendered.

For a moment, I thought Yutz would charge at him and rip him open from the gut. I closed my eyes. I didn't think I could bear to see such horror.

When I opened my eyes, Yutz had hobbled forward with his head bowed, his ears tucked back. He went right up to the other dog and licked his face. He circled him once and then, without any objection from his enemy, he lay down beside the other dog and rested his head across the German shepherd's stomach. He started licking the wounds that he had caused.

I remembered what Michel had told me: "Dogs are not like people. They do not hate."

I watched them together, and I wondered if the German shepherd would let me get close enough to see to his wounds. I was a medic, after all. I had some bandages. Maybe I could save him. Goldsmith would be fine for a few more minutes.

He'd have to be. I couldn't just leave the dog here to die. There had been enough death for one day.

I moved forward slowly, my arms open.

Yutz looked up at me, his dark eyes wide, and he whimpered. He was hurt too, I could see it. But his tail wagged as I approached.

"I think I gave you the wrong name," I told him as I got closer. "You're not a *yutz* at all."

The German shepherd panted heavily now. His tongue hung from his mouth and I could see at least five places where he was bleeding. He growled at me as I approached, but an almost-silent snarl and a quiver of Yutz's lip told him what was what and the German shepherd hushed up. He'd lost his fight and now he had to let me help him.

I pulled some gauze bandages from my shoulder bag, and just as I was about to lay the first one across the big dog's chest, I heard a loud snap by my ear. I ducked and three more came quickly.

SNAP, SNAP, SNAP.

Yutz yelped and fell backward and the German shepherd on the ground flailed once.

It took me a second to realize that the snaps were gunshots.

Everything moved in slow motion. I reached out to Yutz, to touch him, to hold him, to help him, but another *SNAP* exploded into the snow right between us, and I dove back and rolled to see where the shots had come from.

The Nazi dog handler had just killed his own dog rather than let me help him. He'd shot Yutz too. Now he took aim at me, the barrel of his pistol smoking. I saw his eyes blazing, the glimmer of the SS lightning bolts on his collar, and I rolled as he fired again. The bullet grazed my cheek with a sharp sting.

I kept rolling. If he kept firing, I don't know, but when I looked up he had tossed his pistol away and was charging at me with a knife in his hand.

I hopped to my feet and raised my fists, ready to tear him apart. He'd shown no mercy to my friend or my dog. He wouldn't get any mercy from me.

This wasn't war.

It was personal.

BODY AND SOUL

He swiped the blade at my chest, and I jumped back out of the way, but he kept swiping. He sliced open my shirt and stabbed at my heart. His lunge missed, and he fell off balance. I fought the desire to keep moving away from him and his blade. Instead I rushed forward so that I was too close for him to lunge at with the knife again. I slammed into his stomach and knocked his arm aside so that the knife fell into the snow. Then I brought my knee up as hard as I could. He doubled over in pain, and I delivered a sharp uppercut to his chin. The blow sent him staggering back.

I thought I had him beat, and I moved in to knock him down with another punch, but he was no fool. He was carrying a second knife. The moment I stepped toward him, he flung it from his boot.

It zipped through the air just slowly enough for me to see its point shine, but too fast to dodge it.

The blade dug itself into my right shoulder. He'd been aiming for my neck, I guess, and he'd just barely missed. The knife hurt as it went in, and I felt the pain and tingling all the way down in my fingertips. I tried to lift my right arm. I couldn't.

I didn't have time to pull the blade out. He charged and tackled me to the ground, pressing the knife deeper in, all the way to the handle, as we smashed into the snow. His fist cracked across my jaw and I saw stars. He rained punches down on me, and I couldn't lift my hands to block them. My mouth filled with blood; my head spun.

Images came to me in blurry fragments, like the pieces of a dream you remember for only a moment as you wake up. As soon as you catch them, they're gone.

I saw my father at the kitchen table, his tears when I told him I was going to fight the Nazis. I saw Goldsmith in his foxhole, smiling at me, asking if I spoke English, asking about fairy tales, shouting at me to get out of the foxhole to do my job, calling me a *yutz*. I saw the trees exploding with artillery fire, the terrible night I spent with the dead body of my sergeant, the dead body of the Nazi in the foxhole, and

Yutz fighting to defend his fallen master. Yutz drinking water from the canteen in my hands. Yutz letting me sleep on his belly like a pillow. Yutz rising to attack the resistance fighters, Yutz leaping to attack the Nazi on the train, Yutz diving at the other dog, Yutz knocking the Nazi dog handler off of me.

That last image didn't vanish.

It was no illusion.

Yutz had risen and dived at the German, tearing him from on top of me.

"Nein! Nein!" the man shouted, but Yutz did not obey him. He bit and tore at the German's clothes, snapped at his arms as he tried to shove the dog off.

He landed a hard punch across Yutz's nose that sent my dog reeling. The snow turned red where he tumbled, and though he tried to get up again, his paws gave out. He fell. I could see the half a dozen wounds in his side, including a seeping bullet hole. Yutz had lost a lot of blood. He didn't have any strength left in him.

The dog handler climbed to his feet and reared back his leg to deliver a ferocious kick to Yutz's head, a kick that would surely kill him.

Despite the pain, I leapt to my feet, yanking the knife from my shoulder as stood. I screamed, but as I screamed I thrust my arm forward as forcefully as I could and I felt the knife go into the Nazi's back. With all my strength, I shoved him to the side and, at the same time, I twisted the knife. He screamed as he fell and his feet kicked up into the empty air.

He hit the ground and rolled once down the small slope away from the train tracks. The knife in his back stopped him from rolling any farther. His eyes were open, looking up at the sky, and his face held a look of surprise. He died like that, in the snow, surprised, as I stood over him, breathless and bleeding. I knew I had killed him and that everything I had learned growing up said killing was wrong. My training as a field medic had taught me to save lives, not take them. But I had done it, and I have to be honest: I didn't feel bad about it at all. I didn't feel a thing.

Perhaps that's the greatest horror of all. War doesn't just kill and maim and destroy. It numbs, like the cold numbs, but in a deeper place. It numbs the feelings of kindness and mercy and remorse. It freezes the heart. My heart felt cold right then, and I wasn't sure it would ever thaw.

But when I turned to Yutz, I learned that my heart, though frozen, could still break.

It shattered, and those shattered pieces cut. I loved that dog and I knew I could not save him.

Yutz looked up at me, but lacked the strength to lift his head. He whimpered, and I bent down to touch him. My hand came away from his fur bright red.

"It's okay," I whispered. "You're a good boy. It's okay."

I dropped down next to him, holding him in my arms, petting him and whispering in his ear.

I felt his breathing slow. I saw the brightness of his eyes grow dim, like a fire deep inside him had gone out, and a moment later, I knew my dog had died.

I didn't know the things that Yutz had done before he came my way. I didn't even know his name. He'd fought with the Nazis, and maybe he'd done terrible things, cruel and bloody deeds against the innocent and the good. Maybe.

But I'd seen with my own eyes what he'd done since I knew him, and I hadn't a doubt that he died a hero, as much a hero as any soldier who ever fought in any war. It wasn't a good war the two of us were in. I don't know if there ever could be such a thing as a good war, but Yutz was a heck of a good dog in it, and that's no small thing to be. They don't write biographies of dogs or build them memorials of marble in the capitals of the world, but they should.

I wanted to bury Yutz, but my wound wouldn't let me so much as move him, let alone carry him to a suitable place and dig a hole. Besides, I had to get back to Goldsmith. He'd be waiting and worried and freezing, and neither of us was out of danger yet.

I stood and looked down on the black-and-brown mound of fur at my feet. I'd heard it said that dogs don't have souls, so they can't get into heaven when they die. Part of that was true. This dog didn't have a soul.

No.

He *was* a soul. He *had* a body, and he'd let go of it at last. What became of the body didn't matter, not to him. His soul was free.

I smiled then, to think of that, and then I picked up the boots from the ground where they'd fallen, and I made my way back to my friend. Goldsmith and I had a long way to go, but I felt sure that we'd make it. We had a good soul to watch over us, the soul of a dog, and there's no soul better.

COUNTING

That's about all there is to my story.

When I went back to Goldsmith, Hugo was with him. He didn't say anything, and I could see the streaks of tears in the dirt on his face, but he was a tough kid and he had some fight left in him. He offered to guide us to the Americans, and we followed him. It took us the better part of two days to make it back to the American lines.

"Where will you go?" I asked Hugo.

He didn't understand me.

"Your grandparents?" I asked.

He still didn't seem to understand, but he saluted and scurried away toward his ruined village, where I hoped his grandparents would be waiting for him. I never found out what became of him. There were a lot of stories like his in the war, unfinished stories.

By the time we reunited with the American army, the tide of the war had turned. The GIs I had seen retreating along the road that one night had regrouped and attacked on the same day that the air force took to the sky again, the same day I'd led the rescue of the prisoners. They smashed the SS Panzer Brigade to pieces. By Christmas Day, American forces had stopped the German advance, and not long after that, the British and the Americans pushed Hitler's army into a full retreat.

Goldsmith and I met up with a group of paratroopers that took us to some ruined city behind the front lines, where we got our wounds fixed up and got to eat hot food. I'll never forget that first meal. It was the day after Christmas and we got to celebrate. Even Goldsmith celebrated Christmas that year. It was his first one.

"Don't tell my grandmother," he said, laughing.

We got a plate full of hot roast beef and corn and peas and steaming brown gravy, and right on top of it all, a gooey blob of chocolate pudding. I don't think anything ever tasted so good to me as that chocolate pudding on roast beef.

A few days later, when I was rested up, I wandered off from the aid station, and I found a place where they were keeping some German prisoners that had been taken. I wouldn't say they were comfortable, but they got food and water and they were kept in far better conditions than Goldsmith and the rest had been kept.

"Anyone speak English?" I asked at the fence. Most of them were kids who'd probably been pulled out of school to fight in the war. They didn't know anything. But one guy, a German Army officer, stepped forward.

"I speak English," he said.

So I asked him what he knew about the dogs that fought in the German Army. Of course, he'd never heard of a war dog named Yutz. That was the name I'd given him. I never knew the dog's real name.

The officer didn't know much about war dogs, except that they were mostly German shepherds, not Doberman pinschers like Yutz. The officer told me he didn't know of any dogs like that fighting with the German Army.

"We call this kind *teufel hunden*," he said. "Devil dogs. They do not fight with the SS."

"But they do," I told him. "I found him with the SS. He came with me."

The man shrugged. I could see that he did not believe me. "I do not know much," he said. "I am not an important man. I am not a Nazi. You will tell your superiors, yes? Tell them I am not a Nazi. I fight for Germany, not for Hitler. You will tell them, please? I am an innocent soldier."

I walked away from the German officer, even as he kept talking.

"An innocent soldier," he said. I didn't think there could be such a thing. Except for maybe Yutz, my devil dog.

I don't need to give you a history lesson. The Americans and their allies won the war in Europe a few months later. Hitler had killed himself in a bunker in Berlin. On May 8, 1945, the Germans offered their unconditional surrender.

Because of what the government called my "bravery," risking my life to save those prisoners, I was awarded a bunch of medals and got to finish out my service in the army back home in America, touring the country to boost civilian morale. Why the people at home needed a morale boost, I didn't understand. It wasn't like they had to sleep in foxholes or see the things we saw over there, but I did what the army asked me to do, and my parents sure were proud to see me get those medals pinned to my chest. My citation said nothing about a Nazi dog, and the army did not seem interested in hearing my story as it really happened. Just like the German officer, they didn't believe me about Yutz either.

I stayed friends with Goldsmith after the war. He even moved to Albuquerque, New Mexico, to live me near me. He opened a fabric store, just like the one his family had in New York City. He joked a lot about that, a Jew who moves back to the desert to open up shop.

"What would Moses say?" He laughed. I didn't really get it, and Albuquerque isn't the desert anyway, but I laughed too, because that's what friends do. We don't have to always understand each other as long as we can get along. That's the most important thing. If I could learn to get along with Yutz, after he'd tried to tear me limb from limb, well, I figured I could get along with anybody. And that's what I did, my whole life.

I never stopped thinking about Yutz, the best dog I ever knew.

I tried to do some research on those terrible days when he and I shared an adventure. I never could find out about Doberman pinschers on the front lines, but I learned that the surprise attack in the Ardennes forest had been the last German offensive of the war. It came to be called the Battle of the Bulge, because it caused a big bulge in the German front lines.

The attack started early that December morning with

Goldsmith and me in our foxhole, and with thousands of guys just like us in their foxholes all along the front lines in the Ardennes forest, and it went on for over a month. It was the Nazis' last chance to turn the war back in their favor.

It didn't work.

They thought we'd all just roll over when their tanks crushed through, but we didn't. The GIs fought too well, and the generals pushed back too hard for the Nazis to break through. Their whole plan crumbled. The Ninety-Ninth Infantry held their ground. The 106th fought back. The 101st Airborne and the 82nd Airborne stopped the German tanks in their tracks. General Patton's Third Army and General Bradley's First Army cut through the Germans and sent them running back into Germany. The whole attack had accomplished nothing but delaying the end of the war.

That was a hard fact to swallow when I heard it. I was glad we'd won, but I came to learn that nineteen thousand American boys died in those few weeks of the Battle of the Bulge. And even that was nothing compared with over a hundred thousand German soldiers who died or got wounded or just went missing during that same short time. It was a loss of life greater than anything I could have imagined, and it was just a tiny part of a war that killed millions of people.

Twenty-five hundred dead at Pearl Habor. Thirty thousand on Iwo Jima. Twenty-five thousand dead in the firebombing of Dresden. Forty thousand in the bombing of London. Two hundred thousand in Hiroshima and Nagasaki, two million dead at Stalingrad, six million Jews murdered by the Nazis in their death camps, millions more gypsies and disabled people, political prisoners, homosexuals, and others that the Nazi state found "undesirable" and then exterminated.

In total, the Second World War killed almost seventy million people, many of them soldiers, but most of them civilians.

I asked around a bit, but no one counted the number of dogs who'd lost their lives in the war. In battles between nations, I guess, nobody counts the dogs.

But I do, starting with one.

This is a work of fiction, but it is set during events that were all too real.

World War II was fought from 1939 to 1945 between two military alliances: the Axis Powers, led by Germany and Japan, and the Allies, led by the United States, Britain, and the Soviet Union. By the war's end, most of the nations of the world had become involved in violent conflict, making World War II the most deadly war in history, killing between fifty and seventy million people, most of them civilians.

The Battle of the Bulge, also called the Ardennes Offensive, was one of the last major battles of World War II in Europe. It was fought from the morning of December 16, 1944, to January 25, 1945. Adolf Hitler, badly beaten on the Eastern Front against the Soviet Union, believed he could turn the tide of the war if he could break through the American and British front lines in Western Europe, pushing the Allied forces back to the sea. With great secrecy, he mobilized thirteen divisions of over two hundred thousand men against the poorly equipped, inexperienced, and much smaller units of American troops in the Ardennes forest. The Sixth Panzer Division, led by SS General Sepp Dietrich, spearheaded the attack and, as was later documented, committed many war crimes, executing American prisoners and laying waste to towns and villages.

During the Battle of the Bulge, a small group of American soldiers that were taken prisoner, some of them Jewish, many of them simply picked for "looking Jewish," were separated from other prisoners of war and taken by rail to a concentration camp in Germany. There they were forced to do slave labor, and they witnessed firsthand the destruction of the Jewish people in the Holocaust. Among them was Anthony Acevedo, a Mexican-American medic with the 275th Infantry Division. He stayed silent about his experiences in the concentration camp for sixty years before coming forward to share the horrors he and his fellow prisoners endured under the Nazi regime. I was inspired to tell this story, in part, by his real-life ordeal.

While there was great horror during the war, there was also great heroism. The Ninety-Ninth Infantry Division really was surprised by the German attack on December 16, 1944, and many were sent into retreat, but a small group of brave men, vastly outnumbered, fought back and held the Germans off for a full day before being surrounded. This delay gave the Allies a chance to bring in reinforcements and prevent a catastrophe. Individual acts of heroism were common on the front lines too, as regular guys — American soldiers cut off from communication, with many of their young officers dead — acted with bravery and intelligence to protect their fellow soldiers and fight back against the German assault.

In my research, I used many great accounts of these events as experienced by the young men who fought World War II in Europe. Among them were *Battle of the Bulge* by Stephen W. Sears; *The Longest Winter: The Battle of the Bulge and the Epic Story of WWII's Most Decorated Platoon* by Alex Kershaw; *11 Days in December: Christmas at the Bulge, 1944* by Stanley Weintraub; *Citizen Soldiers: The U.S. Army from the Normandy Beaches to the Bulge to the Surrender of Germany* by Stephen E. Ambrose; *The Good War: An Oral History of World War Two* by Studs Terkel; and the most important book written on the history of military working dogs in the American war effort, *Always Faithful: A Memoir of the Marine Dogs of WWII* by William W. Putney. For the train attack scene, I must give credit to my friend Dennis Cahlo, whose knowledge of the films of Steve McQueen remains indispensable. I am also certain that HBO's excellent miniseries *Band of Brothers* influenced this work in countless ways.

At the start of the war, the American military did not have a war dog program, even though dogs had been fighting alongside humans for centuries. The United States developed a program late in the war, calling on dogs donated from the civilian population. People gave their family pets to be turned into soldiers. While many were not suitable, many did serve and returned home as heroes, most notably Chips, the most decorated war dog in the army. He fought in North Africa, Italy, France, and Germany. Mostly, however, dogs were used by the US military in the Pacific theater of operations. The Doberman pinscher was the favorite dog of the Marine Corps, and to this day on Guam, there is a memorial to the brave men and their dogs that fought there.

The German Army used dogs in their military for the entire course of the conflict. Dogs guarded and tracked prisoners, protected bases and supplies, and went into combat.

According to Jan Bondeson, author of *Amazing Dogs: A Cabinet of Canine Curiosities*, Hitler was so fond of dogs and their keen senses that he even developed a secret training program for dog communication, hoping the Nazis could train SS dogs to read, write, and speak with their human masters. Needless to say, his program failed, as, thankfully, did his war effort.

Don't miss the next installment of

DOG TAGS!

Andrew and his hound dog, Dash, hunt down deserters and criminals during the Civil War. But are they on the right side?

History comes alive with these unforgettable war stories!

SCHOLASTIC

scholastic.com

SCHOLASTIC and associated logos are trademarks and/or registered trademarks of Scholastic Inc.

MNIA

Four teens. One war.

From National Book Award finalist Chris Lynch

"Lynch puts his readers in the center of intense conflict, conveying what it feels like to face a largely unseen enemy."

—*Booklist*

SCHOLASTIC

scholastic.com

Available in both print and eBook editions.

SCHOLASTIC and associated logos are trademarks and/or registered trademarks of Scholastic Inc.

VIET